THE LEGACY SERIES

The Spirit in My Shoes
John Michael Cummings

The Effects of Urban Renewal on Mid-Century America and Other Crime Stories
Jeff Esterholm

What Makes You Think You're Supposed to Feel Better
Jody Hobbs Hesler

Fugitive Daydreams
Leah McCormack

Hoist House: A Novella & Stories
Jenny Robertson

Finding the Bones: Stories & A Novella
Nikki Kallio

Self-Defense
Corey Mertes

Where Are Your People From?
James B. De Monte

Sometimes Creek
Steve Fox

The Plagues
Joe Baumann

The Clayfields
Elise Gregory

Kind of Blue
Christopher Chambers

SIGNS OF THE IMMINENT APOCALYPSE

"Bell's storytelling skills take many forms, making her hard to pin down. In her first collection, she deftly moves from retelling fairy tales to crafting her own brand of gritty realism. Some commonalities here include memorable explorations of the passage into adulthood and stunning portrayals of nature—few writers can describe a fox sniffing the air quite so lovingly—especially where the wild butts up against the man-made. In one story, a girl captures a gopher to keep as a pet, but the fear of rabies takes over. In another tale, a man is convinced that his body lit up when he landed on a hive of bees. Bell also successfully dabbles in satire. Her title story is a genre-defying list of the many ills of our modern world, including, on the fashion front, the return of the cowl neck as a sure sign of societal collapse. This biting humor exists alongside tender moments such as a father learning how to tell a bedtime story. With her mix of light and dark, lovable and unlikable characters, and hope and regret, Bell's collection is part Neil Gaiman and part Donald Barthelme, with a touch of Joyce Carol Oates."

—*BOOKLIST*, starred review

"An exquisite, achingly rendered collection of stories. Heidi Bell's recipe is part fairy tale, part biting social commentary—hopelessly romantic with a sharp edge. Though the book is raucously funny, Bell knows how difficult life is—and how incompetent most decent people feel as they navigate it—and she pushes her characters to their limits, because the way through is the hard way."

—BONNIE JO CAMPBELL
author of *The Waters* and *American Salvage*
finalist for the National Book Award

"A dark seen-it-all humor animates Heidi Bell's portraits of women and men of the American urban Midwest—she knows their frowsy self-esteem, their good-natured shame at where they've ended up, their excuses, and that simmering envy of those who have it easy that only rarely connects to a pathway out of their own bad situations. Bell knows American women and men, and she knows her way around the American language, from its jazzy and cornucopial top to its dank, bump-and-grind bottom. It seems there's nothing that Heidi Bell can't do, with her earthy wit and cunning imagination, encyclopedic resources of language, and deft mastery of literary forms, from short-short to classic long to modal in-between. Most of her stories center on the so-called real world that makes us laugh and wince, and yet a golden thread of magic, shape-shifting, and light along the edges is also at play in these stories, often allowing a glimpse of another world altogether, the richer universe where stories are born. This is a versatile, highly readable collection."

—JAIMY GORDON
author of *Lord of Misrule*
winner of the National Book Award

"Heidi Bell is one of our great unsung writers. Let these stories sing to you. Listen to their music and you will fall under their spell as I did."

—MATTHEW SALESSES
author of *The Sense of Wonder*

"A fierce and funny collection from a highly original and enchanting sensibility. Bell's stories X-ray our psyches in the way fairy tales do—revealing essential motivations while also shining a brilliant light on the marvelous, the disturbing, the uncanny. Her hardscrabble women and broken men fight on, often despite having one hand tied behind their backs by wrenching backstories. Beauty and yearning blend with terror and depravity in these artfully written pages."

—ANDY MOZINA
author of *Tandem*

SIGNS
OF THE
IMMINENT
APOCALYPSE

SIGNS

OF THE

IMMINENT

APOCALYPSE

AND OTHER STORIES

HEIDI BELL

CORNERSTONE PRESS
UNIVERSITY OF WISCONSIN-STEVENS POINT

Cornerstone Press, Stevens Point, Wisconsin 54481
Copyright © 2024 Heidi Bell
www.uwsp.edu/cornerstone

Printed in the United States of America by
Point Print and Design Studio, Stevens Point, Wisconsin

Library of Congress Control Number: 2024937559
ISBN: 978-1-960329-43-1

"Striped Gopher" © Monica Friedman. Used on the cover by permission of the artist.

This is a work of fiction. Names, characters, businesses, places, events, and incidents are either the products of the author's imagination or used in a fictitious manner. Any resemblance to actual persons, living or dead, or actual events is purely coincidental.

Cornerstone Press titles are produced in courses and internships offered by the Department of English at the University of Wisconsin–Stevens Point.

DIRECTOR & PUBLISHER
Dr. Ross K. Tangedal

EXECUTIVE EDITORS
Jeff Snowbarger, Freesia McKee

EDITORIAL DIRECTOR
Ellie Atkinson

SENIOR EDITORS
Brett Hill, Grace Dahl

PRESS STAFF
Carolyn Czerwinski, Sophie McPherson, Kylie Newton, Natalie Reiter, Angelina Sherman, Holly White, Ava Willett, Cam Williams

For Adam

CONTENTS

ANGELS

The brightest of lights and a liquid dark presence, a smell like smoke and mussels gritty with sand, motion over water streaked with moon. He remembers the reverence in his mother's voice as she told him how it was said that she would have no children, and then, unexpectedly, one summer day so hot it wilted the leaves on the trees, the angels brought him here.

As he grew, his body caught up with the large toddler's head that, in the albums full of photographs, seemed as out of proportion as a sunflower on its thin stalk. And as he got older, he learned things that made him doubt his mother's stories, things about human anatomy and what desire does to it. Snickering in health class, he held the condom with two fingers, flung the diaphragm like a Frisbee to the boy at the next desk, pretended to eat all of the tiny multicolored birth control pills in the white plastic case. He spent his years at Jefferson Junior High slouching through the hallways with boys who bragged about what the easy girls gave up outside the gym during school dances. He knew how he had gotten here. He had read the words and seen the diagrams. He had even heard his parents at night.

Still, he could not shake the myth, could not attribute to storytelling or imagination the sensations of the elements bound together inside him, the feeling of flying at incomprehensible speeds, his body's earliest and truest memories. He swam beneath the surface in ponds and lakes, even in the public swimming pool with his eyes open, looking for a doorway, the home of the angels he knew had made him out of mud and shells and carried him, scorching, into the air. Sometimes after his parents had gone to bed, he would climb out his bedroom window to the flat porch roof, light a Camel he had stolen from his father's secret stash, look out to the dark water of the glittering lake just beyond his yard, and listen for splashes, watch the sky for streaks of light.

When he was seventeen, there was a girl for whom he felt a wrenching nameless emotion. Together, they swam off his parents' dock one night in August to escape the heat emanating from the trees and grass, heat trapped by the heavy cloud cover. Automatically, he swung his arms back and forth under the surface of the water, waiting for a touch, a slick form to brush past him in greeting; he searched the perimeter of the lake, the sky above the trees.

The girl's hand startled him when it rose from the water and reached for his shoulder, which she pressed once before turning and swimming to the ladder. He followed and lay on his back next to her, the warmth of the wooden dock soaking through his towel. They talked about the rest of the weekend, about homework and dinner with her parents on Monday. Don't be nervous, she said. She leaned over his body, and the dragging ends of her wet hair brought goosebumps to his skin. And when she kissed him, on her lips, on her tongue, he tasted his beginnings: water; salt and algae; sand crystallized by fire.

AN EASY MEAL

The animal envoys of the Unseen Power no longer serve, as in primeval times, to teach and to guide mankind. Bears, lions, elephants, ibexes, and gazelles are in cages in our zoos.

—Joseph Campbell, *The Way of the Animal Powers*

I

In the beginning—and still—Fox dances in his black stockings, following Bear, always just out of Bear's reach. His nostrils sip the air, his only waking impulse the mouth-watering curiosity pulling him forward to the hindquarters of a deer sunk in a bed of pine needles or to the ripe, delicate layers of rotting fish buried in the bank of red sand. Bear's secrets give way so sumptuously beneath Fox's paws. He is exquisitely attuned to Bear, feels the air quiver when Bear turns again toward one of his caches, and Fox slinks away.

When the berries dry up and the snow sifts down through the trees, Bear disappears, and it's a matter of principle for Fox to follow the thread of a scent on the cold air, to steal into Bear's den. The redness of him, his intricate musk trickle into Bear's dreams, and Bear moans as nimble black lips grasp and sharp white incisors drag a rabbit carcass from a cocoon of dried grass out into the snow.

Fox and Bear dream through the long winter nights as the Storyteller at the fire describes them in tales conceived while watching from the patient underbrush, praying for god to appear as a fat buck. Stories of Fox pilfering Bear's honey, Bear's fish; Fox tricking Bear into ice fishing with his tail, formerly bushy; Bear insisting, in tale after tale, that might is superior to wile—proven wrong again and again.

II

Spring is when it rains and rains, and—like the stream that thaws and swells and overflows, moving everything in its grasp onward through space and time—the Storyteller, alienated now from the forces that made him, reaches in and makes a mess of things. Fox lunges for an easy fish but is caught in the roiling water and buffeted by the churning debris of Nature and Civilization—gravel, shards of clay pots, broken branches, the twisted frame of a loom, clots of winter leaves, a cracked coat of arms, a sodden map of the British Empire.

The Storyteller deposits Fox, weak and battered, far downstream. The unfamiliar forest reeks of Bear. The smell is coming from a heap of rocks, a castle, toward which Fox creeps until the door bangs open, and three male Bears emerge on hind legs, dressed in cloak, in tunic, in doublet and pantaloons. As the Bears step onto the path, their front paws dangle idiotically. Fox is pulled after them as if attached by a string, unsteady and disoriented, for he, too, is walking on hind legs, his nose exceedingly far from the ground, his luxurious tail wagging with unease.

The Bears notice him there and approach, and Fox cowers inside the sensory overload of them, three boar Bears together. He bows low, drawing his foot back along the ground in keeping with a custom that has nothing to do with him but has somehow taken over his body, and the Bears grunt with laughter and call him "Scrapefoot" before going on their way.

Where has it gone—Fox's supple ability to evade capture? In this unholy place, any of the Bears could have torn him to pieces while he bowed and scraped. For the first time, he wants to be free of Bear, and he wrests himself out of the invisible grip of the Storyteller, who has decided all animals must now walk upright. Fox hunches now on all fours and feels more himself. And as the scent of the Bears fades, he is compelled to fumble with the door latch and slip inside the castle, for where Bear is, there is an easy meal. He ransacks the place, searching for the caches, but the Storyteller— unfathomably—has stashed nothing in the cushions lining the three thrones of rock, nothing in the wardrobe but cos- tumes for dancing—red wool jackets, feathered hats, iron nose rings on long chains.

Finally, a delicate scent from the dining table: three bowls of milk. Fox dips a paw and licks. The first too sour, the second too sweet, the third just right, and he laps it all up. Then, swollen and milk drunk, he stumbles toward the ban- quettes along the wall and curls up on the one layered with leaves just right.

His senses deadened by the milk and the thick walls of the castle, Fox is unaware of the storm stirring outside, of the Bears' return, even when they exclaim, "Trespasser! Thief!"

He wakes only when they have him by the legs and are swinging him out the window and into the whirling wind.

III

And when The Storyteller finally drops Fox to the ground again, he finds his fur flattened by swaths of cloth that smell of Civilization, a scent adjacent not to delicious rotting things but to a creature that has died long ago and dried to a husk. There is something on Fox's head, slipping down into his eyes—the Storyteller has dressed him with a nest of gray hair.

Someone kicks him in the side, *oof*. He tastes blood, smells fire, and looks up, terrified, at a man wearing a black coat, brandishing a stick.

"Can't stay here, old woman," the constable says, holding his nose, and Fox stands unsteadily on hind legs.

He has been hijacked completely now, gone from brother, mentor, god drawn on the cave wall to an object of suspicion, disgust, scorn. The Storyteller spots a Fox loping along the edge of the woods and sees a tricky chicken thief, a fur stole. An indigent old woman comes weaving out of the forest, a mirror of the Storyteller's own failures, and he thinks *witch*. Fox totters away from the constable, in among the trees, his movement constricted by skirts and cloak.

Not far into the woods, a little stone house, and again, as though they've been waiting for him, three boars troop out, this time dressed in striped and flowered and checkered waistcoats with pocket watches. They hardly smell of anything now, more prop than animal. Tap, tap, tap, go their walking canes along the lane toward town.

Fox watches from behind a tree, cold in spite of his clothing, his stomach gnawing at itself. He'll never catch a rabbit in this getup. Drawn to the little house inevitably, instinctively, in spite of past disappointments, for where there's Bear, there's food. Inside, however, the only edible thing is a small bowl of sticky gray gruel. But at least he can curl up in a warm bed.

He wakes to the Bears' bellowing:

"A stinking vagrant! Call the constable!" says the great huge Bear.

"Let's burn her alive!" says the middle-sized Bear, with a gleam in his eye.

"Let's throw her out the window!" says the little small wee Bear.

IV

Once again, out the window—and into the midst of a miasmic cloud of creativity born in a human city. It gathers strength and mass over the river bobbing with the sewage and junk necessary to Civilization. The cloud carries Fox along until the Storyteller reaches in and plucks him out, throws him into a thicket far from the home he remembers and longs for with all his senses.

He is wearing a short childish dress now, which his tail can't help but lift in the back, exposing his haunches. He draws his testicles up even tighter against his pelvis, to keep them safe. The Storyteller has changed the nest on his head to one of golden hairs that curl every which way and interfere with his peripheral vision. He peers out from the thicket into a clearing wherein stands a little house.

Again, three Bears come out, this time a boar, a sow, and a cub, dressed as father, mother, and child. Fox's mouth fills with saliva, and he waits, drooling, for the boar to kill the cub and eat its meat. He scans the landscape to anticipate where the boar might cache the carcass. Instead, the Bears set out together at a jaunty pace along a path through the woods.

Inside, Fox ransacks, eats the paltry offering, and sleeps, only to be awoken by Baby Bear's high-pitched voice in his ear.

This time, to Fox's amazement, he escapes before even one curved black claw can graze the sash around his waist. An inkling of hope, then, that he might escape this story, this Storyteller altogether.

"I hope you've learned your lesson!" Baby Bear shrieks after him as Fox dashes on all fours into the forest.

Fox's stomach growls as he puzzles over what the lesson might be—perhaps that these Bears are not Bears at all. He crawls under the low branches of a dogwood to shed the golden wig, snags the sash on raspberry thorns, gnaws through the waistband of the dress and leaves it draped over a log. Then he lifts his nose, tastes the air, sinks into the place inside him of Knowing, and sets off for home.

THE SIDETRACK

By three a.m., the last of our Fourth of July guests had gone home, and Ben and I were lounging drunkenly on the couch we had carried down from our apartment for the party, along with a loveseat, some chairs, and a decrepit wheelchair Ben had found on the curb on garbage day and brought home. Ben was reminiscing about the home run he'd made during Wiffle ball when a rusty white pickup careened into the parking lot next to our three-flat and stopped nowhere near any of the demarcated parking spaces. It was the same truck I'd seen two days before, crammed with furniture. From our kitchen window, I'd watched two men—one large, one small—carry lamps and a couch, a mattress and a bed frame into the vacant first-floor apartment.

Now, the small man, with the streetlamps on him like overlapping spotlights, fell out of the passenger side of the pickup and, maintaining his balance like a tightrope walker, managed to make it to the wheelchair parked in our ragged circle. The tall bearded man emerged from the driver's side and strode toward us, hiking up his pants by a belt loop.

"Larry Hart," he said, offering his hand to Ben while looking at me. "I moved in the other day."

I'd expected a bass, but Larry's voice was a raspy tenor. He had a smallish beer gut and longish hair that left only a hint of earlobe visible. His beard climbed high onto his cheekbones.

Ben's blond forelock bounced as they shook hands. "I'm Ben," he said, "and this is Annie. We live on the second floor."

Larry gave me the manly handshake, which not all men do; instead, they give you the tips of their fingers, and they don't squeeze, as if they think they might hurt you.

"Please, have a beer," I said, gesturing toward the half-barrel with the flourish of a game-show tart.

"You two married?" Larry asked, one eyebrow disappearing beneath his bangs.

Ben and I laughed, as we do. "We're just friends," I said.

"Allow me to introduce The Weasel," Larry said, tipping his head toward the smaller man.

The Weasel waved limply from the wheelchair.

At the half-barrel, Larry sucked down a cup and refilled it before carrying one over to The Weasel, who took it but then put it down on the ground and started rocking and rearing up in the chair.

"Our buddy Mouse can sure get around in one of these things," The Weasel said. "He can pop a wheelie like nobody's—" He tipped over backward and lay silently on the blacktop with his feet in the air. He had kicked over his beer, and the puddle crept stealthily toward him like the Blob.

Larry made no attempt to help his friend.

"Is he okay?" I asked.

"Phttt," Larry said.

The Weasel's legs twitched, and I could hear him breathing loudly, so I figured he was alive, at least.

"Mouse's legs were severed by a train," Larry said.

"Oh my God!" I said. "What happened?" I leaned forward. I could feel the corners of Ben's mouth twitching.

"He came in for a few beers one night when I was tending bar," Larry said, giving me his full attention. He stroked his beard, and I felt blood rise to the surface of my skin. My sundress suddenly felt too short.

"I'll admit he was quite inebriated when he left. But I'm a bartender, not a babysitter."

"Yeah, you are," Ben said.

"Besides, he was on foot," Larry continued, "and he only lived a few blocks away, adjacent to the railroad tracks. Still, some people blamed me."

Larry rubbed one of his thick hairy forearms, and I thought of Bluto, Olive Oyl's dark temptation.

"Mouse had always found his way home before, walking along the tracks," Larry continued. "But that night, for some godforsaken reason, he passed out lying right on them. He doesn't remember anything after leaving the bar. The engineer saw him from a few hundred yards and engaged the emergency brake. When he realized he wasn't going to be able to stop in time, he unlocked the wheels, and they cut right through Mouse's legs. The metal was so hot, it cauterized the wounds, which saved his life. Otherwise, he would have bled to death."

Ben slapped my bare knee with the back of his hand, trying to get me to look at him, but I didn't dare. "It cauterized them!" he said.

Larry pushed back his mustache and drank the rest of his beer.

GENE, OUR LANDLORD, HAD BEEN renovating the tall narrow three-flat since before Ben and I moved in, and we had imagined once, when stoned, that we were living in an unfinished drawing. When I opened the door of our apartment and walked out onto the second-floor landing, I sometimes felt as though the floor had been sketched in just in time for my foot to land on it, the drywall drawn in over the studs, sheet by sheet. But when my mom visited, she couldn't help literally pointing out all the housing code violations—a cracked window here, a hole in the wall there, sagging floors, a broken faucet, a growing water stain on the ceiling. She had worked so hard to keep us out of shitholes like this. What was I doing, living here in squalor?

Ben and I still felt lucky to have found the place. The rent was right in our price range—ridiculously low—and included heat and electricity. Ben was doing body work for the mechanic who'd apprenticed him and who now sometimes couldn't afford to both pay him and keep the garage open. I had graduated from the university in May with a bachelor's degree in behavioral science, which, according to the counselors at the career center, qualified me for a job as a behavior technician, someone who tells people with disabilities or old people in nursing homes what to do. Or, with my accumulated knowledge of human behavior, gleaned from the psychology, sociology, and anthropology classes I had taken out of genuine interest, I could work for a marketing company, finding the right angle to persuade people to buy protein powder or massage chairs.

My mom hadn't gone to college, and she'd planted in me the idea that a college education would open the world to me like the automatic doors at the mall. I hated to prove her wrong.

"What is your dream job?" the career counselor asked, her pen poised over the form on her clipboard.

"Um," I said. Was providing running commentary to *Forensic Files* a viable career? "How about a forensic scientist?" I said hopefully.

She quickly looked down at the clipboard. I could tell she was trying not to roll her eyes. I felt set up.

"I'm certain you need a master's degree for that," she said without looking up. "And chemistry."

I wasn't sure if she was commenting on my lack of college credits or lack of charisma.

"Are you interested in applying to graduate programs?" she asked.

I wasn't sure.

SOON AFTER LARRY MOVED IN DOWNSTAIRS, The Weasel moved into the two-bedroom flat above us. On the days I wasn't working, I could hear him pacing up there and talking to himself. Often his language seemed to disintegrate into snarls and grunts. He laughed a lot, too, high and nervous like, well, a weasel.

One Friday night, Ben and I walked up the street, as we do, to the Argonaut Bar, on the border between our shabby neighborhood and the Capitol Square. Gene also owned the Argonaut, and he regularly gave Ben and me a handful of beer chips. Larry had started bartending there, and Ben and I came through the door that night just in time to see him—a bottle of 151 dangling from one hand—light his Zippo and breathe fire. The flames shot out three feet from his mouth, and a roar of appreciation rose up from the barroom. We were apparently living sandwiched between a wereweasel and the devil himself.

At bar time, Ben and I fell in with the migration of students and hipsters; drug dealers in cowboy hats and businessmen in gleaming dress shirts, their breast pockets leaking neckties; downtown secretaries and hookers, hard to differentiate sometimes in their makeup, short skirts, and spike heels. All on their way to one of Larry's parties. Larry's friend Hector had a key to the apartment, and he let everyone in while Larry closed the Argonaut. Hector was also the designated DJ, and he played funk, disco, and Mexican ballads with the bass so loud that the windows vibrated in their frames. Upstairs, Ben and I listened or turned the TV up loud. Larry never invited us to his parties, so we didn't go.

Another night, another party on the first floor. Ben and I clomped up the front porch steps to find a lumpy horizontal shape on the couch there. It was a homeless lady we'd seen collecting cans from the garbage in the back. She lifted her head and stared at us. She had popped-out eyes and iron-gray hair like a dozen steel wool pads stuck to her head. Her belongings were lined up neatly against the yellow siding, next to her wire shopping trolley.

"Larry said it was okay," she said to us, and then she lay down again and closed her eyes.

Ben and I looked at each other and nodded decisively, as we do. Then he unlocked the security door, and we walked in to find a couple struggling passionately in the dark vestibule.

"Oh, my lord," Ben said and shielded my eyes from the sight as we went laughing up the stairs.

Larry's parties didn't bother us. Ben could sleep through anything, and I was a night owl. If I lay down before I was exhausted or on the verge of passing out, my mind went straight into the fun house, where a different terror waited around each corner: How long before my mom would stop sending checks? Would the gorgeous girl I kept seeing at the Argonaut ever look my way? Was I wrong to hold out, to not just get a job at a fast-food restaurant? Was I doomed to be a behavior technician? How would I ever pay off my student loans? Behind one door, my mom's voice over the phone. Behind another, the way she looked fearfully over her shoulder when walking to her car in my neighborhood. I wanted to say, "It's okay, Mom, they're just hookers. They won't hurt you—unless you want them to."

It was easier to block out these thoughts when I filled the summer days with amusements—swimming out to the raft at B. B. Clarke Beach or, if someone had a car, taking a road trip to Devil's Lake to hike or swim or take mushrooms and talk about how the tumble of rocks at the foot of the bluffs didn't quite seem to have come to rest yet or, after dark, watch the stars swirl in the black water. Everyone wanted to stay in Madison after graduation, and that made it difficult to get a job there, even if you knew what you wanted to do, and, as the summer waned, the friends I'd graduated with disappeared, one by one. Nicole ended our summer fling by taking a job as a case worker for the department of children and families in Milwaukee; Raj and Ingrid moved to Minneapolis to start a master's program in psychology; Damon started law school in Ann Arbor. It seemed so easy for them, their paths visible while mine remained shrouded in darkness.

ONE SWELTERING LATE-AUGUST AFTERNOON, I came home to find the gorgeous girl from the Argonaut sitting on our front porch. She had short blond-tipped dreads that flared out around her face like the sun's corona. Her eyes were honey-colored, and I was willing to bet that, close-up, they were flecked with green. The overall impression was that she'd been dipped in gold. Whenever I saw her at the Argonaut, she was with a hella thin, hella pretty Black girl. My friend Nicole had grown up with Golden Eyes, whose real name was Camille, in the Marquette neighborhood, and Nicole knew Camille's girlfriend as Baby Dyke, a nickname she'd gotten at Rod's, the gay bar in the Hotel Washington. I rarely went to Rod's, because so many of the butch lesbians there gave us bi girls the side-eye and refused to dance with us, much less date us. We had it easy, they said, because we could pass in the straight world.

Golden Eyes looked out of place on our porch, sitting on the arm of the tattered brown couch in dark dress pants and a long-sleeved white shirt. She didn't appear to be sweating, though her long sleeves were buttoned at the cuffs, covering the tattoos on her arms.

"Hey," she said, standing. She was several inches taller than I was and slender. She shifted her weight nervously as I came up the porch steps. My heart soared to think she might recognize me. Then she said, "I'm looking for Weasel. He live here?"

"Yeah. Third floor."

I pressed The Weasel's doorbell and then unlocked the security door and held it open for Golden Eyes. I followed her up the stairs, admiring her muscular back. With every step she took, gilded wallpaper appeared, progressing up the wall of the stairwell. I was kicking myself the whole time for being so tongue-tied. The Weasel's head appeared over the railing above us. Golden Eyes froze.

The Weasel grunted. "You Camel?" he asked.

"Yeah," Golden Eyes said. She followed The Weasel up the stairs to the third floor as though she were on her way to the gallows.

The Weasel sold a lot of cocaine to the bank execs and the legislators' staff up on the Square. Golden Eyes was dressed as though she worked up there, but I wondered if she had realized before now that drug running was an unwritten job requirement. I had no argument with coke; it's nice to feel invincible for a few hours. I liked that feeling so much, it was probably a good thing I could only ever do it on someone else's dime.

I stood in the open doorway of my apartment, and, after a minute or so, I finally thought of a decent invitation to try out when she came back down the stairs: "Want to come in for an iced coffee?" But then Camille came flying down as if a wereweasel were on her heels. She didn't pause on the landing or even glance at me.

I tried to shrug it off. She had a girlfriend, and earlier that day at the unemployment office, I'd met a guy, Charles, who seemed nice enough and was decent-looking, if slightly buck-toothed. While filling out the paperwork on our respective clipboards on opposite sides of the room, he and I had looked up at the same time, and our eyes met. When we smiled sheepishly at each other, I felt a spark, I guess—maybe something like what happens when you flick a lighter that's running out of fluid and you're just praying that it lights one more time to fire up your bong.

Very soon after we met, I found out that Charles had a beautiful body. He practiced yoga and read books about yoga and meditation, which he had lots of time for, seeing as, like me, he didn't have a job. He also had a luxurious deep voice, and sometimes I liked to feel it roll over me. But he was bossy, insisting I become a student of his smallest habits. When we were having lunch at the Argonaut one day, for instance, he set his cheeseburger down carefully in the center of his plate and said, "Notice how I save all my milk until the end of the meal so I don't fill up on it?"

I nodded slowly, biting my tongue hard to keep from laughing.

"Oh, snap!" Ben said after meeting him. "He's so *old!* Daddy complex much?"

It was true that I'd never met my dad, who left when I was a baby.

"I guess I'm an optimist," I said.

"Yeah, you are," Ben said.

I did wonder sometimes if it was optimism or something else that compelled me to ignore whatever misgivings I had about a situation. Or maybe it was more like a willful suspension of disbelief. My decision to go out with Charles had been based mostly on inertia. The first time he touched my breast, I consciously decided to interpret the jolt that passed through my body as desire rather than alarm.

"You can't fault me for wanting to believe in love," I said to Ben, and then we burst out laughing.

Ben and I have known each other since high school, and we're as close as a brother and sister. We've considered becoming romantically involved, but each time the subject comes up, something just isn't right. The previous December, during my winter break, we'd holed up for a marathon session of bong hits, bad television, and foods boiled in oil. During *The Adventures of Hercules*, Ben crawled across the floor toward me. The whites of his eyes were pink, and he had an unnatural smile on his face. Apparently, he was turned on by the fight Hercules was having with a villain in a pointy metal bra. I had just eaten the last french fry and was in the process of tearing some toilet paper off the roll to wipe away my oily mustache.

"Do you want to fuck at all?" Ben asked.

I gazed into his bloodshot eyes with real regret. "I'm just not feeling that sexy right now, you know?" I said and tried unsuccessfully to suppress a roiling belch.

The night Charles's and my relationship ended, Ben had gone to O'Cayz to listen to some punk/noise rock bands. It all started when Charles tried to take my diaphragm out.

"What the hell?" I scrambled out from under him and stood next to the bed. "Do you want me to get pregnant, you idiot?"

"Listen," Charles said quietly, running the fingertips of one hand back and forth over his fabulous pectorals, "if you ever. Ever. Call me an idiot again, I will knock. You. Out."

His words caused me to freeze in place, naked with my hands on my hips. Then I shivered, as though waking from a nightmare. My heart was pounding so hard I thought he might be able to see it. I took a couple of careful steps back, reached down to the floor for some raggedy shorts and a T-shirt and put them on.

Charles was still talking softly, a lilting rhythm to his words. "I don't want to feel that thing between us when I'm making love to you. I don't want anything to come between us. You know, the first time you smiled at me, electricity shot up from my root chakra and out my third eye." He smiled dreamily, baring his slightly buck teeth, but then the smile straightened out. "I wonder now if you have the slightest idea who you're dealing with."

I decided then that it actually did matter to me that Charles had been in prison, even if it was only for drunk driving. That's what he said it was for anyway.

"Are you finished?" I tried to sound calm.

"Yes," he said and yawned like a cat.

"Good," I said. "Now get out."

Charles sighed heavily but made no motion that suggested leaving, so I left the room and closed the door behind me and tried to breathe and slow my heart rate. Why did I have to be so impulsive? Why didn't I ever think things through? Now I regretted not putting on nicer shorts or even pants so I could just walk up to the Argonaut. I considered calling the police. Charles was on probation—did they put people on probation for drunk driving? —and he would go to jail for sure if the cops came. I wasn't sure I wanted that on my conscience. I left the apartment and went down the front stairs, thinking I'd sit on the porch awhile with Mrs. Prescott, the homeless lady. Maybe Ben would come home soon.

In the entryway, I could hear a ball game on in Larry's apartment. Stopping there in the dark, my heart pounding, I thought of all the times I'd stumbled out of my childhood room after a nightmare and run down the dark hallway to crawl into bed with my mom.

I gathered my nerve and knocked on the door. Larry opened it. Black hair sprouted from the neckband of his spotless white T-shirt.

"Hello, neighbor," he said.

I crossed my arms over my chest. I hadn't thought to put on a bra.

"Hi, Larry," I said. "I have a sort of problem. There's a guy in my apartment—"

"Say no more." He let the door fall open, and maybe it was the adrenaline, but as he did, an invisible hand seemed to fill in the vivid details of the room behind him—the rich brown wallpaper and its gilt detail, the gleaming hardwood frames on the tall windows, the glowing green plants hanging in front of the windows and crowding the shelves and tables.

Gene had certainly gotten farther on the rehab down here than in our apartment.

"He was invited and everything," I said, tearing my eyes away from the fat leaves of a huge jade plant. "It's just—"

Larry held up one hand, and I closed my mouth. I watched him pull on a pair of greenish-gray snakeskin cowboy boots and arrange the legs of his jeans over them. I had never seen him wear shorts, no matter how hot it was.

He opened the hall closet and pulled out a metal baseball bat, and together we went upstairs and found my bedroom empty and the back door wide open. Charles had apparently slipped away down the back staircase.

"Well," I said to Larry, who stood in the middle of the sloping kitchen floor, leaning on his bat, "thanks for coming up here."

"Where's your roommate tonight?"

"He went to see some bands, which often leads to meeting a girl . . ."

Larry scratched underneath his beard with one hand and eyed me, while I wondered what he had in mind. I'd had enough excitement for one night.

"Well," he said, "why don't you come down and have a beer and watch the game?"

How could I say no after he'd been so willing to hit someone with a bat—or at least threaten him with it—on my behalf? "All right," I said.

I had him wait while I put on some underwear, and a few minutes later I was sitting on the rug in front of his coffee table, drinking Busch from a bottle while he rolled a joint. I scanned his bookshelves, which were crammed with paperbacks—Bantam editions of *Le Morte Arthur* and *Great Expectations* and *The Scarlet Letter,* along with mysteries, true crime, and science fiction.

"You okay?" Larry asked.

"Fine." I felt strong and jumpy. My muscles twitched under my skin as though I'd been running.

"I didn't like the look of that guy when you brought him into the Argonaut," Larry said. He licked the edge of the rolling paper.

My eyes slid away from his pink tongue. I was a bad judge of character, sure, but I still didn't like anyone calling me out.

"I knew a girl a few years back, called Cat," he said. "We worked together at the Sentry warehouse—I worked inventory and she drove forklift. She'd been doing it since she was a teenager." He lit the joint and sipped the smoke. "We used to say she had balls," he choked out and then blew out a cloud. "Someone would challenge her to swim across a river and she'd say, 'Let's go,' even if she'd hardly swum a stroke in her life."

Larry smiled and squinted through the smoke that curled up around his face. He told me that by the time she was thirty, Cat had done everything. Bungee jumping, skydiving. He saw her so wasted on quaaludes once she had to crawl across the floor on her stomach to get to the bathroom. She was in the hospital for a couple days after a drinking contest with a bouncer. Then she started going out with a guy who was too much like her. Their idea of a fun Saturday night was getting high and playing Russian roulette or going a hundred miles an hour on the freeway in his sports car. One night they clipped the bumper of another car, rolled, and burst into flames.

Larry snapped his fingers. "Both of them, dead." He pulled in more smoke from the joint and then finally held it out to me, his eyes glittering. "Have you ever woken up someplace, with someone, not knowing how you got there?"

He knew from my expression that I had. I accepted the joint and took a few hits, using the smoke as an excuse to close my eyes.

"You put yourself in danger," he said, his voice quiet, "and sooner or later, something bad's going to happen."

"Am I in danger right now?" I asked, just as quietly.

That made him laugh, the raspy tenor belly-laugh I'd heard so many times through the floor late at night.

What I couldn't tell him was that if I was like Cat at all, the similarity was only a surface one. I didn't put myself in danger on purpose—I was just stupid. I looked like an adult, and I was expected to act like one, but most of the time I felt like an idiotic child who didn't know how to navigate the grownup world. I didn't even really know what a quaalude was.

I woke up the next morning in Larry's La-Z-Boy recliner, covered with a crocheted brown, orange, and white afghan, beer bottles clustered next to the chair like bowling pins. Larry's bedroom door was closed, but I could hear him breathing loudly in his sleep.

CHARLES STALKED ME AFTER THAT ENCOUNTER, calling several times a day. After the first few calls, I stopped answering the phone. His attempts to contact me were alternately threatening and sweet, sometimes both at once, like when he sent flowers with a card reading, "Bitch, return my calls." The messages on the answering machine were all some version of "We are meant to be together; just accept it." Listening to them filled me with regret and a sense of my own stupidity, so I began hitting the erase button as soon as I heard his voice. I felt too ashamed to be afraid. Maybe I deserved to be stalked after being so easy.

Two weeks later, Ben and I were on our way to the Argonaut, swinging our clasped hands between us, as we do, when we crossed paths with Mrs. Prescott. She was pushing the little wire shopping trolley full of her belongings, presumably headed to our porch for the night. We said hello, and she stopped in her tracks and fixed me with her popped-out stare.

"Careful," she said, and a dirty finger emerged from the sleeve of her sweater. She pointed it at me like the witch from a fairy tale. "Your other boyfriend has been lurking outside the house. I told Larry about it."

"Okay, thanks, Mrs. Prescott," I said, dismayed but not surprised. I had seen Charles around—at my regular bus stop, outside the unemployment office—but so far, I'd always spotted him before he saw me. I looked back over my shoulder now, wondering if my luck was about to run out.

"Maybe it's time to call the police about old Chaz," Ben said as we continued up the hill.

When we got to the Argonaut and talked to Larry about it, he agreed, and I told them I'd go to the police station around the corner the next day.

I was just waking up around noon when I heard the phone ring. I leaped out of bed and picked it up before the machine could.

"Annie, finally," Charles said wearily. "I'll be right over."

"No, Charles, you're not coming over! We are not getting back together! And if you're still on probation, I suggest you stop calling—" He tried to interrupt me, but I just kept talking. "—stop sending letters, stop lurking outside my house, all of it! Once more, and I'm calling the cops."

He hung up on me. Weeks went by without a word from him, and Mrs. Prescott said she hadn't seen him around. Ben and Larry were annoyed with me for not going to the police, but I figured Charles had gotten the message.

IN OCTOBER, THERE WERE SO MANY temporary holiday jobs available that I had to take one as a clerk in a store downtown. Trinkets was stuffed to the brim with high-end crap that only people with too much money would buy, from crystal snow globes to teak doll furniture. There was so much junk crammed into that little shop that I could never find anything I was looking for. It didn't help that many of the fragile items were packaged in plain white boxes in a stockroom with floor-to-ceiling metal shelves. My coworker Loretta, the other temp, watched me one day from the doorway, playing with the end of her long braid, as I scaled a shelving unit like Spiderman.

"What are you looking for?" Loretta asked in her baby voice. She had a master's degree in philosophy, a voice like a four-year-old, and was working for six fifty an hour. She was nice enough, so why did I want to kill her? I knew why I wanted to kill the customers, entitled people full of unreasonable requests. I thought I might go on a killing spree if I heard one more person in a sheepskin coat say something like, "It was right here in the window when I walked by two weeks ago. It was blue and about the size of my hand."

"I don't think I'm cut out for retail," I told Ben. "I just don't have the patience to deal with rich people as though I give a shit."

"Hush now." Ben put his arm around me. "You just haven't found your niche yet. But I agree, it's not retail. Now, what time do you have to be at work tomorrow?"

"Not until one thirty, actually," I said.

"I've got just the thing then," he said, squeezing my shoulder. "Let's go up to the Argonaut. We're out of beer chips, so wear something tight, and we'll see if we can get a free drink out of Larry."

Three days a week I had to be at Trinkets at eight thirty in the morning, an hour I had rarely seen during the past five years unless I'd stayed up all night. I tried to go to sleep early but only flopped around in my bed, the doors in the fun house in my mind opening all the way down the long corridor. I would read in bed awhile, then get up and pace in tandem with The Weasel on the third floor, and finally fall asleep at two or three o'clock, only to have the alarm blast me awake at seven fifteen. The early morning light made me squint in an unattractive manner, my eyes puffy and piglike. By my third week at Trinkets, I was strung out.

But I rallied the night I saw Golden Eyes at the Argonaut without Baby Dyke. Ben massaged my shoulders like a prize fighter's coach as I tried to get up the nerve to talk to her. Then he pushed me down the bar toward her, and I bumped into her elbow. Smooth. She turned to look at me with her sleepy golden eyes.

"Hey, hi," I said.

She considered me, nodded slowly in greeting.

"Can I buy you a drink?" I asked. I needed one myself, to stop my legs from trembling.

"Sure," she said in her husky voice. She stepped sideways to make room for me next to her at the bar.

Over a beer, she told me she was going to MATC for an associate's degree in human services. She hoped to be a school social worker one day. She had had a really good one at her elementary school when she was a kid. As I'd suspected, she was working as a messenger at the Capitol to put herself through school, doing clerical work and running errands for legislators in the general assembly.

When one of her friends interrupted us to say that they were leaving to go up to Pinckney Street Hideaway, I held my breath.

"That's okay," she said to them. "I'll see you later." We talked a little while longer, and then she leaned in close. "I'm thinking of going home," she said. "Do you want to walk me? It's just over on East Johnson."

On our way out, we passed Ben at the bar. He held up his hand for a high five, and I ignored him.

Camille's apartment, the downstairs of a two-flat, was almost as bad as ours—stinking carpet, peeling paint, a cracked windowpane in the front door—another rental in the student ghetto, but I would've bet they were paying more than we were. In the living room, two of Camille's roommates were playing Super Mario Bros. on a big old console TV, the electronic theme song turned up loud. Camille lifted her hand toward them in greeting and then continued down the long hallway and into one of the bedrooms. She invited me to sit down on the bed and then went and got some beers from the kitchen.

"Do you like coke?" she asked as she opened a jewelry box and took out a baggie.

"Yeah," I said.

We did a few lines and each drank a beer and jumped on the bed and talked about how great Julianna Margulies was on *ER* and laughed uncontrollably, and then had the most electric, ecstatic sex I had ever experienced. Then a few more lines, another beer, more sex, and then my own voice echoing in my head as I chattered away.

"You would not believe how much money these rich assholes spend at Trinkets," I said. "Hundreds of dollars on tchotchkes that have no real *purpose*. I mean, really, what is the use of an Italian art-glass duck figurine? What could it possibly *mean* to someone?"

Camille was laughing, a low staccato like the most enchanting gun I'd ever heard. I grabbed her shoulders and looked into her golden eyes. "Tell me!" I said, also laughing.

We slept for a few hours and then went to breakfast at Cleveland's, both of us sore and sheepish and hungover. We exchanged phone numbers, hugged on the sidewalk, and went our separate ways. It was a given that I liked her more than she liked me, so I fought the urge to call her over the next couple of days, but daydreaming about her made my work shifts sail by.

LATER THAT WEEK, AFTER FALLING ASLEEP relatively early out of sheer exhaustion, I woke at 3:17 to the pulsating music of one of Larry's after-bar soirees. Downstairs, people were talking and laughing, and each time I put my head back down on the pillow, mariachi music spiraled up through the springs in my mattress.

After twenty minutes, I stomped into the dark kitchen, fished the spider-web-covered broom from the crack between the refrigerator and the wall, and began pounding on the floor with the handle. The talking downstairs stopped momentarily, and I heard Larry laugh, high and hoarse. Someone down there answered by pounding on the ceiling.

"Hey, Annie!" Larry called. "Come on down here, sweetheart!"

"I'll come down there, all right, you inconsiderate pig," I muttered, going to the back door with the broom still in my hand, not caring that my hair was matted and I was wearing only a T-shirt. I hoped Camille wasn't down there. I didn't want her to see me like this.

When I opened the back door, someone was there, standing on the landing in the dark. We both shrieked and jumped back. The door to the storage room across the hall was open, and light from the streetlamps in the parking lot poured in through the windows, silhouetting a short lumpy figure. I felt around for the kitchen light switch and in the subsequent glare recognized Mrs. Prescott.

"Oh, hi," I said. The smell of her reached my nostrils—sort of a mixture of vomit and hot tar. How long had she been sleeping in the storage room? Come to think of it, I had heard some scrabbling around in there when I took out the garbage, but I'd assumed squirrels had gotten in. "You can't sleep either, huh?"

"No," she said softly. "I went downstairs an hour ago and asked Larry very politely to be more quiet but he laughed at me! How rude!"

"That bastard!" I shook my broom. "I'm going down there."

The bag lady stared at me, her Muppety eyes unblinking. I noticed a greenish light coming from her hand and saw she had flipped open a cell phone. She tapped out a number on the lighted keypad. Who could she possibly be calling?

"I'd like to lodge a noise complaint," she said into the phone.

"What?" I shouted. "No!"

She ignored me. "This is Mrs. Prescott." She recited our address as though she'd been living there for years.

"Whhhy?" I asked beseechingly after she hung up. I resisted the urge to fall to my knees. "Are you trying to start a civil war?" I began to pace in The Weasel's pattern—three steps diagonally across the kitchen, three steps back. "What do the cops do for a noise complaint?"

"I believe they simply tell the offending party to be quiet," Mrs. Prescott said, tucking her phone somewhere among her many garments. "Without reasonable cause, they can't even enter the apartment."

I looked out the window. A squad car was already pulling into the parking lot. They must have been harassing prostitutes just down the block. As two officers strolled up to the house, hands on their nightsticks, I began pounding frantically on the floor with my broom handle. This time there was no response. The music pulsed on.

Mrs. Prescott and I listened from the top of the stairs as the music stopped abruptly, and the cops at the back door lectured Larry on consideration for one's neighbors. In the silence after their departure, I waited, cringing.

"*Hey!*" Larry's voice echoed hugely in the stairwell. "Whoever called the cops is *dead*! You hear that, Prescott?"

Mrs. Prescott froze with her hand on the doorknob to the storage room. Her mouth began to tremble.

"Goddammit, Larry!" I shouted down the stairs. "Some of us have to work in the morning, you fucking—"

"And I don't need any horseshit from you, Miss Day Job!" Larry slammed his door so hard the entire house shook.

"Do you want to sleep on our couch?" I asked Mrs. Prescott. I held the broom tightly to control the shaking in my hands.

"No, thank you."

"Don't worry. Larry wouldn't hurt you." At least I didn't think he would. Probably not tonight, anyway.

Mrs. Prescott smoothed down her top skirt—a tartan plaid. She backed into the storeroom. "Well, goodnight," she said. She shut the door, and I heard the lock turn. I'm not sure why a storage room would lock from the inside.

Throughout this whole ordeal, I hadn't heard a thing from Ben's room. When I peeked in, he was snoring, as he does, with the fan on high and his size-twelve feet sticking out from under the comforter.

The next morning, I was getting out of the shower at seven thirty when someone knocked on the front door. It was Larry, looking like hell. Even his beard seemed hungover.

"What do you want?" I said, turning away and rubbing my dripping hair with a towel. "Why aren't you asleep?"

"Why in God's name would you allow that woman to use your phone?" Bruised-looking bags swelled under his eyes.

"I didn't," I said. "Believe it or not, she has a flip phone. I tried to stop her, and I tried to warn you! Didn't you hear me pounding? You act like you own this house, but there are other people who live here too. And I told you I'm having a hard time getting up for this stupid job!" I was so tired and agitated, I could have cried.

"Annie," Larry said, his hands clenching at his sides. "A friend of mine by the name of Wolf was arrested last year for possession of fifty grams—grams! —of cocaine and some prescription tranquilizers. Sentenced to five years. While he was in prison, he killed a guy in self-defense, and now he's in for life. That's not going to be me, sweetheart. Can you understand that my guests and I were in a compromising situation when those cops came to my door?"

"When aren't you in a compromising situation?" I said, but I regretted it immediately.

Larry looked hurt.

"I told you," I said, "I tried to warn you. And now Mrs. Prescott is probably on the run, thanks to you."

"Actually, she's downstairs having some coffee," Larry said.

"Oh."

"The smell of her might just drive me around the bend. I'm going to try to get her to take a shower. I'll see you later." Larry sighed and then lurched down the stairs, his hand dragging along the water-stained wallpaper.

BABY DYKE AND CAMILLE HAD BROKEN UP FOR GOOD, it seemed, and Camille and I went out a few more times in

November and early December. We had a few beers, did some coke, and went dancing at Rod's; had a few beers, did some coke, and went ice skating at Tenney Park; had a few beers, did some coke, and stayed in. I bought the beer and gave her what money I could for the coke, but I was starting to feel uneasy about how she always had some. Why did she always have some?

December twenty-fourth would be my last day at Trinkets, and, like a little kid, I was counting down the days until Christmas. My mom couldn't believe they would make me work on Christmas Eve.

"What are you thinking about doing with your life, Anna?" she had asked at Thanksgiving as her boyfriend served himself another helping of potatoes and looked at me with his eyebrows raised in honest interest.

"Um," I said, feeling stupid, "I'm not sure. I do know that retail sales is out of the question." I smiled goofily, but my mom only managed a strained smile in return.

At Trinkets, the manager worked weekdays, so Loretta and I were often stuck working weekends eight thirty to five or one thirty to ten. On a Saturday night in the middle of December, Loretta poked her head into the stockroom and said, "I'm going to lock the door."

"Okay, thanks," I said.

We had been hella busy that day, but it had started snowing around eight, and business had slowed. In that quiet interlude, I made a list of the tiny gift books that needed restocking and went to the stockroom to find them. We sold more of them than anything else, but I couldn't figure out who actually *read* them. When I heard the bell on the front door tinkle, I thought fleetingly of Charles, and my heart started to race.

I peeked out the stockroom doorway and was relieved to see someone in a parka with the hood up and a scarf around their neck, someone too slender to be Charles, thank God. This late customer said something to Loretta in a quiet voice, too quiet for me to hear, and then, head lowered, followed Loretta down the long counter toward the stockroom. Loretta saw me there, peeking out the doorway, and I noticed that her face was a strange color—bluish-white, like cream cheese. She looked straight at me and then cut her eyes, and I almost laughed, because she was always so nice to everyone, even the rudest, most disrespectful customers. The late customer didn't see me there, and I instinctively ducked back inside the stockroom. Is that what Loretta had been directing me to do? She walked around the counter, and, surprisingly, the customer followed her back there, all the way back down to the cash register. Was it someone Loretta knew? Her husband coming to pick her up? He had never come to pick her up before. Why didn't I just step out there and ask?

Because something was wrong. I watched as the customer pulled the backpack off his back, pulled a gun out of it, and pointed it at Loretta.

I lurched sideways and crouched down against the stockroom wall. My pulse disappeared and then kicked in again unevenly, as if tapping out an SOS in Morse code. There was a phone in the back corner of the stockroom. Would the robber hear if I called the cops? Thank God the Muzak was still on, playing "Let It Snow" for the hundredth time that day. I picked my way carefully, silently through hundreds of white boxes of expensive junk and picked up the receiver. The 911 operator had a hard time hearing me.

"There's a guy here with a gun," I whispered.

"Where are you ma'am?"

Where was I? My brain wasn't working right.

"In the stockroom at Trinkets."

"What's the address?"

"I have no idea. On State Street." It took an unbearably long time for me to explain where the store was located. Was it the two hundred or the three hundred block?

"Are you in immediate danger?"

"Uh, yeah!" I said. "But not as much as Loretta!"

After I hung up, I just sat in the stockroom for a minute. How long would it take them to get here? What if they couldn't find us because of my shitty directions? What if he hurt Loretta while I hid back here like a coward? My vision had gone funny, as though there were a piece of yellow cellophane over my eyes. Without really knowing what I was doing, I took an armful of the gift books I had gathered and walked out into the store.

"Hey, Loretta," I called, "I found more *Cats and Dogs*, but no *Love Letters*—"

The cash register drawer was on the counter, empty. I couldn't see Loretta. The robber turned and looked at me with her golden eyes and pointed the pistol at my chest. It was Camille. I hadn't recognized her because the Camille I knew wouldn't be caught dead wearing jeans and a parka.

"Hey," I said. I thought I might vomit.

"Hey."

My eyes moved from her beautiful face to the gun. What was she doing? What would happen to me if she pulled the trigger? Would she ever pull the trigger? Depending on where she hit me, blood would probably splatter everywhere, along with tissue and probably some bone. I thought of Larry's friend Cat playing Russian roulette. But that's not how she died.

I found my voice. "What are you doing? If you're in trouble, we can find some other way—"

"Come back here." Her husky voice so soft and gentle. I stepped behind the long counter and walked down to the register. When I reached Camille, she took the gift books from me and set them down on the glass countertop.

Loretta was on her knees crying in front of the safe. She looked up at me, her eyes wide and blank with panic. "I can't remember the combination," she said. "I just can't remember it."

"Keep trying." Camille was strangely serene as she wrapped silver duct tape around my ankles and wrists, but waves of heat were coming off her, carrying a sharp metallic odor. Her calm scared me more than if she'd been sweating and shaking, like I was. The maroon carpet began to pulsate with my heartbeats, and I felt so high, I thought my head would explode. Fear as hallucinogen, I thought. If I could bottle it, separate it from actual danger, I'd be rich. I almost laughed.

"You don't have to do this," I said. "There's still time to just—"

"Shhh," Camille said. "You have to stop talking. I don't want anything bad to happen to you."

My blood ran cold. When the cops came, would they shoot her? Would we end up in some kind of hostage situation, like in a TNT movie? I didn't want to think I'd seen my mom for the last time. I thought of Ben, who was probably sitting on the couch right now cutting his toenails and letting the clippings fly all over the rug, preparing for the hot date he had tonight with a cute woman whose car he had fixed. I thought of Larry breathing fire. If Larry were there with me, he would talk Camille down, make her leave without the money before the cops got there, and then later, in his stories about it, he would give her an animal nickname, maybe Tiger.

I thought about these things to keep from dwelling on the fact that this was all my fault. I should have asked Camille about the coke, shouldn't have done it with her, shouldn't have mentioned Trinkets and all the cash we had at the end of the night.

The lock on the safe clicked loudly. "Oh, thank God, thank God," Loretta said. Camille stuffed her backpack with bills from the safe and taped Loretta up. When she walked out the door, the bell tinkled.

"Don't worry," I said to Loretta. "I called the cops from the stockroom."

"Oh, thank God, thank God," Loretta said, as though these were the only words she could remember. We stared at each other until the shouting started outside, and then we looked out through the glass display case and past all the crap arranged in the front window. Camille was there, her cheek pressed up against the gold R in TRINKETS.

We heard someone jiggle the door, but it had locked behind Camille. A few minutes later, we heard the lock break, and the bell over the door tinkled merrily. The sound made me want to scream.

"Hello?" a woman's voice called.

"Back here," I yelled, "behind the counter!"

A handsome butch cop with a dark moptop appeared. "Don't worry, ladies," she said. "Everything's under control."

Even though it was over, Loretta started bawling, and I almost did. The adrenaline was wearing off, and my hands were shaking so badly I had to wait awhile before I could write down an account of what had happened on a yellow legal pad, as the other cop, a short guy with red hair, requested. The butch cop, Officer Zieger, asked if we knew anything about a second person, an accomplice. Driving up the block with their lights off, before Camille had even come out of the store, they'd seen someone else lurking outside. He ran when he saw the cop car. Officer Zieger described him as about five ten, a hundred seventy-five pounds, wearing a long dark trench coat.

"Um," I said and told her about Charles, feeling lucky to have dodged one literal bullet and one figurative one. Then I told them that I knew Camille, and they had me write that down too. As I wrote it, I was filled to overflowing with regret.

Loretta's husband came to pick her up, and Officer Zieger gave me a ride home in her squad car while her partner collected evidence at the store.

"You did a good job tonight," she said. "You really kept your cool."

"Uh, what?" I said, bewildered. I was colder than I'd ever been, shivering inside my down coat as though I were wearing only a T-shirt, even though I could feel the squad car's heater blowing against my shins.

"I'll let you listen to the 911 tape sometime," Zieger said. "Have you ever thought about becoming a cop?"

I was sure she was just trying to make me feel better—or maybe she was just trying to make me. I laughed, and it came out sounding high and goofy, like The Weasel.

In the parking lot outside my house, Zieger handed me her card with our case number written on the back.

"I circled my phone number," she said, and we exchanged a look. "You really should consider applying to the law enforcement program," she said. "I'm not kidding. Oh, and we'll find your ex-boyfriend. Tonight."

It was reassuring in the moment, but as soon as she drove away, I was sorry I'd let her go. All the windows in the three-flat were dark. The Weasel and Larry were probably at the bar, and if everything worked out for Ben, he wouldn't be home tonight. I couldn't make myself go inside, couldn't get past the feeling that Charles might be lurking just past the security door or behind my couch or under the kitchen table. The hairs on my arms and legs stood up, sensing movement on all sides. I didn't want to be this one small body, unprotected and all alone.

I trudged through the snow up the hill to the Argonaut, glancing back over my shoulder every few seconds. The noise and smoke inside the bar choked me, and when people's glances touched me, I felt as though they would leave bruises. I found The Weasel at the bar. We nodded to each other. Larry turned from the cash register.

"Annie!" he shouted. He slapped the man who was sitting next to The Weasel on the shoulder, and the man vacated his stool without question. Larry and I leaned toward each other over the bar; I hugged his neck, and he kissed my cheek. His beard was scratchy and infused with smoke. "What's going on?"

"Somebody tried to rob the store tonight," I said, resting my elbows on the bar.

"No! Are you okay?" Larry grabbed my upper arms as if to support me, and I thought he might lift me off my stool.

I looked at The Weasel. "It was that girl who came by the house to see you. Camel."

"Camille?" Larry said.

The Weasel's eyes opened extra-wide.

"Didn't I tell you she was skimming?" Larry said to The Weasel.

"Shit, man," The Weasel said. "She's going to narc me out." He grabbed his coat and disappeared out the door on wave of cold air.

Larry set a tap beer in front of me. I leaned in and said in his ear, "I guess we should have a little housecleaning party tonight, eh?"

"You got that right," he said.

I pondered who might babysit the three-foot bong and other assorted illegal items currently residing in Ben's and my apartment.

I stayed at the Argonaut until after bar time, watching Larry wash glasses. As we walked home together, I figured we could take almost anyone who might come at us out of the dark.

Larry said, "Do you think you'll be able to sleep?" He opened the security door, and we lingered in the entryway.

"Nah," I said. "I have visions of beautiful drug-addicted lesbians dancing through my head."

Larry caught my neck in the crook of his arm and pulled my head against his chest. "Desperation comes in all shapes and sizes, my dear."

"We were dating, you know," I said.

"I know," he said. "I'm sorry."

I told him about my guilty feelings, my regrets.

"You're not responsible for her actions," he said, and I nodded. "But I do wonder why you keep putting yourself in these situations."

"Honestly, I'm just stupid." It felt good to confess.

He laughed shortly. "It's a pretty good excuse," he said, "but I'm just not buying it."

He unlocked the door to his apartment and let it fall open. Inside, he flipped a switch, and golden light spilled out into the vestibule.

More than almost anything, I wanted to step into Larry's apartment, curl up in his lap, rest my head against his chest, get lost in the sound of his heartbeat. To feel safe.

But it was time to grow up, to take care of myself, to make a plan, however daunting. Maybe I didn't want to be a cop, but I could enroll in chemistry the next semester at MATC and see how it went. Maybe I did want to go to graduate school. And maybe it would be okay to work a shit job while I figured it out.

I didn't know if I was capable of these things. I wondered how I had even made it through college. All of my accomplishments seemed to have happened so long ago and far away.

Larry leaned on the doorjamb. "Are you coming in?" he asked.

I shook my head. "I'll be all right," I said, hoping it was true. "Thanks for everything."

I grabbed the worn wooden banister and began to pull myself up the stairs. One by one, the treads appeared like magic under my feet.

SIGNS OF THE IMMINENT APOCALYPSE: A–Z

ADAGES: According to ancient wisdom, time flies when you're having fun, and as the clock winds down to the end of time as we know it, we would do well to have a little less fun and pay attention to the prophecies couched in the old sayings. "Play with fire and you're going to get burned," for instance, contains a prescient reference to the carcinogenic by-products of industry that have depleted our ozone layer and caused both climate change and unprecedented cases of childhood-onset asthma. Likewise, "A bird in the hand is worth two in the bush," should serve as a reminder that you won't be cashing in your evanescent stocks and bonds on Judgment Day! Consider "A stitch in time saves nine," and "Even in laughter the heart is sad, and the end of joy is grief." And what, in this postmodern age, could be more chilling than "Just wait until your father gets home"?

BORDERLINE PERSONALITY DISORDER: We are losing our sense of order, our borders. In the refrigerator, on the Roommate's jar of pickles, you leave a fluorescent pink sticky note reading, "I use the left side of this refrigerator." You hope the Roommate has placed the pickles on the left side of the refrigerator by mistake, that the pickles have not crossed the left-right axis of their own accord. If you don't keep her things separate from yours, you might mistakenly confuse her food, her clothing, her body for your own. You could wake up one morning in the Roommate's bed, wearing the Roommate's pajamas, having dreamt the Roommate's dreams.

CANCER: Nature's calling card, which reads, "I am smarter than you. This message will self-destruct." The Grandmother bounces like a human yo-yo for years between remission and wild cell activity, losing her left breast, a piece of her skull, most of the bone from her right hip. She can't decide which side of the civil war she's on, and when it comes time to surrender the body, she can't unclench the mind. She dies white-fisted, a bald, growling animal.

DYNASTY: An American saga—no less dramatic than the acclaimed television series—now syndicated, rerun, rebooted, an endless loop of the trials and tribulations of the Chosen Families, who—although their offspring prove themselves dishonest or promiscuous or out of touch with reality or poor students at Yale or Harvard or Penn—continue to populate the upper echelons of political life. Is it Fierce Determination, Pluck, Untapped Potential or, perhaps, some outside force that transforms the next generation from Elite Antisocial Dunces to Business Leaders to Governors/ Members of Congress to Presidents of these United States?

ELECTROLYSIS: The decomposition by electricity of body hair.

FASHION: There is nothing new under the sun. The cowl-neck sweater and leggings, painter's pants and overalls have come back on the fashion-go-round, illustrating entropy, American culture collapsing in on itself.

GEOLOGY: Once, along the California coast, dust settled into layers to eventually become stone. Then the stone was ripped up, twisted, and thrown toward the ocean by an unfathomable force—hence, the San Gabriel Mountains. Nearby, the most famous American fault line looks much less dramatic, innocuous as the seam on a tan dress. Note the houses built on either side of the San Andreas, as though it were a picturesque mountain stream. Someday the tectonic plates that meet here but are trying to move in opposite directions will finally spring past each other, and the streets on either side of the San Andreas will no longer match up. How will the children find their way to school?

HEGEMONY: Sounds suspiciously like "Gethsemane." Money changers in the temple. Indignity. Betrayal. "And . . . that ancient serpent . . . the deceiver of the whole world . . . was thrown down to the earth, and his angels were thrown down with him" (Revelation 12.9). Beware the rulemakers.

INFRASTRUCTURE: Tree roots under your street like the tentacles of a Jules Verne creature, uncoiling in super slow motion. Slender blades of grass push up out of the ground so slowly you hardly notice them cracking the sidewalk in front of your house.

JETSAM: Hypodermic needles, oil, plastic bottles ride the ocean currents to the beach. The water from the tap looks clear to the naked eye, but the microplastics and microbes swimming in it plug into your cells just right. For weeks the city's raw sewage has been mixed by mistake with the drinking water. The chlorine probably killed most of the germs, the City Water Spokesperson reports on the radio while you clean your dishwasher and washing machine filters, which have become clogged with toilet paper and feces.

KARMA: An anonymous source reports that the entire population of the United States shall die a violent, fiery death when all motor vehicles simultaneously crash—into one another, into mountains, buildings, trees, and telephone poles. The exact date for this event is TBA, though it has been noted by a Trusted Official that, on said day, no Sport Utility Vehicles will be allowed into Heaven, as they usually only contain one person and thus take up more than their fair share of room in the parking lot.

LEXICON: Our undoing coded into our very language. Written language irreparably wounded by impatience and insufficient education. "Night" becomes "Nite"; "though" becomes "tho"; "through," "thru." Coming Soon: "Deri Delite" and "Kwik Trip" in English-language dictionaries the world over.

MIRACLES: With the other pilgrims, you flock to see a statue of the Virgin Mary weep milk, then trot down the block to witness an old man's stigmata. *Chicken Soup for the Soul* books about angels sell like hotcakes, year after year. The Catholic Girl wears her bra to bed each night because her mother tells her it will keep her breasts from sagging.

NARCISSISM: Three stories of a flower: First, Persephone could not resist its albino flesh, but when she reached out to pluck it, a chasm opened in the field, and she was carried off to the Underworld. Second, the boy Narcissus pined away for love of himself until a flower grew in his place at the water's edge. And now, more recently, weaving in and out of traffic in your Ford Expedition, relishing the desire to drive up and over the Honda Fit ahead of you in the fast lane, you're stuck listening to the list of side effects for the latest psychoactive medication. These small things add up—endless advertisements, slow traffic, slow secretaries and waitresses, slow children and dry cleaners and gas station clerks. These things don't just happen, they happen to You, impeding Your Progress, interrupting Your Focus, which is small and fragile as a flower.

OBESITY: Here in the Land of Plenty, we are very, very hungry. "Starving," you whisper as your Dodge Caravan creeps forward in the McDonald's drive-through lane, your unconscious urging you to grow large enough to contain everything you feel. Afterward, you drive home to your subdivision, where your five-bedroom home still smells faintly of paint and caulking and the cornfield that once grew there.

PANDEMIC: There are too many of us. We stay away from each other, to keep from murdering/dying. "That's all right," Virus says from the top of the food chain. "We'll wait." In our antiseptic rooms, behind closed doors, we are so lonely we could die.

QUAY: Why pronounced "kee" when it looks like "kway?" (See also "Lexicon.")

RELIGION: Muslim extremists, Christian nationalists, Christian missionaries in Cameroon, civil war in Egypt and Syria, Gaza in ruins, India smoldering, Indonesia torn asunder, etc., etc. Isn't it comforting to discover, then, that right here in the United States of America, God has sacrificed his only son so that you might have a place in Heaven? You, a handsome teenage member of the Baptist Church, are guaranteed a place in Heaven, despite your love of Southern Comfort and Coke, cigarettes and marijuana, your love of diddling as many girls as possible in your church youth group—three so far. "I love Jesus," you say warmly, smiling as though into a camera, because isn't He always watching? "Because of Jesus, God will forgive me. In fact, the peace I feel in my heart right now tells me He already has."

SEDITIOUS CONSPIRACY: George Washington strides forth on his magnificent thighs into the Great Experiment, followed across the centuries by little boys wearing grown men's bodies: the self-appointed Patriots. Crying snot-nosed tears for lost causes. Possessed by an inconsolable self-serving peevishness. They are armed and dangerous. They are the tip of the spear that puts out their own eyes. "They are blind guides. And if a blind man leads a blind man, both will fall into a pit" (Matthew 15:14).

TRUSTAFARIANS: A Sophomore at Your State University takes a trip to the University Bookstore, where she piles the counter with insignia clothing under which lies a textbook for Psych 100 and a package of highlighter pens in four neon colors. She pulls her Mastercard from her Coach bag, and the eagle hologram in the silver rectangle catches the light, blinding the cashier for a moment. His squinting makes her laugh. "I call it my Daddy Card," she says, tipping the card and blinding him again. The world is her oyster, her lady-in-waiting, her trash can. She is a Future Young Businessperson of America. When she reaches Wall Street, the Loop, Silicon Valley, the seas will boil, and the moon will rise red.

UNIDENTIFIED FLYING OBJECTS: The danger is in believing too little. You think I'm joking.

VIAGRA: Flying in the face of Nature, male sexagenarians, septuagenarians, even octogenarians all over the world are pressing their erections into their thirty-something wives' backs. Their sperm hobbles on tiny walkers toward the wrinkled ova, thereby propagating armies of unnatural beings, children of the beast: "And the beast that I saw was like a leopard. . . . One of its heads seemed to have a mortal wound, but its mortal wound was healed, and the whole world followed the beast with wonder. . . . they worshipped the beast, saying, 'Who is like the beast, and who can fight against it?'" (Revelations 13.2–13.4).

WETLANDS: When it rains heavily, the water seeps up out of the ground and into the storerooms at the mall. The parking lot floods, and ducks arrive to swim. This place is marked in their memories and in the memories of their ancestors and their offspring. They know in their bird bones, in their DNA, what belongs here and what will be here again.

XENOPHOBIA: In the age of diversity, equity, and inclusion, you have conveniently transferred your fear of

The Other to beings from outer space. Relax! We might just learn something by welcoming the inevitable alien visitors rather than fighting them. We might even be instrumental in establishing a whole new species!

YODELING: While it might just seem like a lot of yelling, this relentless, throaty, and automatic response in certain God-fearing people indicates the presence of the beast, and its proliferation will mark our last days. Listen carefully and you can hear it already, faintly, there behind your mother's voice on the phone line, a backdrop for the music on your favorite Spotify station.

ZOMBIES: You have probably already passed one on the street or in the corridor at work. You probably responded to its granite stare by looking at your phone or your shoes or the wall, or nodding and saying, "Hi." Remember the pock-faced boy running the cash register at the Hilltop Citgo? The indigent woman who wanders around downtown in a cape? As the final days approach, zombies' public appearances will increase. Even more people will claim to have seen Elvis, Malcolm X, and Mary Queen of Scots, and they won't be mistaken. At Lucille Ball's press conference, the star's lipstick will be poorly applied, making her famous mouth appear crooked, taped on. As Shakespeare delivers a speech live on CNN, College Freshman will rub his patchy beard and say, "I thought he was dead." You won't have to put clean sheets on the bed in the guest room when your mother arrives unannounced, her heels blistered from walking in the too-tight shoes in which you buried her.

GOPHER

They're drowning out gophers on Gordon's hill. Mr. Gordon drags a green hose through the backyard, forcing the grass to bare its yellow roots. He shoves the end into a hole in the ground. I crouch on the shady side of the garage, imagining the gophers and their blind, naked babies paddling as their rooms fill with brown water.

Leo Gordon comes out the back door, cramming the last of something into his mouth, the sun jackknifing off his white-blond hair, just like his dad's. I press my cheek against the cool pink siding of their garage, knowing Mr. Gordon's white Archway truck is inside, surrounded by stacks of cookies in clear plastic packages. My mouth waters just knowing how close they are—the fat, soft lemon-iced, the sugar cookies whose huge granules gather between my fingers. Mrs. Gordon serves them at Bible study, where we read aloud obediently, though some of us will never believe.

From two houses down come the Johns boys and their stepfather, Dick, tromping uphill through the backyards. Billy Johns positions himself at a gopher hole with his shovel, and while he waits for a glimpse of the small sleek head, the striped and freckled back, I pull strings one by one from the hem of my cutoffs. My sister runs past me, doesn't notice me there at all. She joins the men and boys, squats at another hole, squinting in the sun, her hands twitching inside two Wonder Bread bags. She is determined to have a gopher as a pet.

I do not want to see the gophers washed from their holes, do not want to watch the men and boys kick their limp bodies into the tall weeds that border the back of the long yard, but I can't seem to leave the shadow of the garage and go home.

Mr. Gordon and Dick stroll over to test the concrete cones they poured around the clothesline poles last weekend. The yard is their place. Inside their houses, they are good only for reading newspapers, for replacing faucet washers and carving meat from bones. Dick kicks a clothesline pole with a black work boot—he wears them even in summer. He examines the pole with small black eyes so mean they can scare your bladder into squeezing tight when he looks at you.

Billy Johns shades his eyes and tracks two teenage girls riding their bikes up the road. His younger brother Marcus kneels at another gopher hole with Leo Gordon. I will go wherever I can to look at Marcus—filthy slit-eyed boy with a mouth the color of Red Delicious. He and Leo are pushing and pulling a stick in and out of the hole, in and out, laughing. Marcus is eleven and banned from our yard for telling my sister and me the joke about a boy named Deeper and his teacher. Now, his and Leo's giggling attracts Dick's attention, and he strides over and slaps Marcus across the head. When Marcus flinches away, Dick slaps him again, harder, and Marcus slinks across the yard to stand on the sloping ground behind Billy.

Just then something pops up near Billy's shoe, and Billy lifts the shovel high to smash it, but on the backswing, he catches the left side of Marcus's face by mistake. Marcus's hands fly to his eye, and red appears in the cracks between his fingers as if the sun or a flashlight were shining through. He howls, his lips the rim of a wet hole. My mouth is open, too, my breath coming fast and damp against my hand as I probe the closed lid of one eye, wondering how much pressure the eyeball underneath might withstand before bursting.

Marcus's yelling voice is unfamiliar, as if other people were talking through him, as if someone were turning the dial on a radio: first he cries, *Mama, oh, no, Mama* like a little boy, and then he screams, *Jesus Christ* and *Shit*. Billy and Dick each grab him under an armpit and hustle him down the hill to his mother's house, and I am drawn to my feet, as if to follow them.

Instead, I search the hill for gophers. Perhaps this is just the diversion they need to escape, to make new lives for themselves in the tall weeds. Then I see that my sister has trapped one in her hands. Wild teeth rip through the spotted plastic of one of the bread bags and catch the soft web between her thumb and forefinger. Still, she does not let go, holds the gopher with both hands until I knock on the Gordons' back door and Mrs. Gordon comes out to scold her for touching the dirty animal but still gives us an old metal toolbox to put it in. While Mrs. Gordon washes the gopher bite and sprays it with Bactine, my sister insists she will keep the gopher in her old hamster's cage. One morning she called me into her room to show me that Buttons was dead by poking the stiff curled body with the eraser-end of a pencil.

My sister carries the gopher home triumphantly in the toolbox, a tissue pinched in the crook of her hand, bright spots of blood seeping through. I follow her down the hill through the afternoon haze that makes the car bumpers and streetlights glitter. I imagine the gophers' revenge: Marcus Johns cries out as the doctor pushes a needle and thread through the skin around his eye. His mother stands beside him, holding his hand, her face tense with his pain. In the waiting room, Billy Johns sits in a chair and stares at the floor. Out of the corner of his eye, he can see the tips of his stepfather's black boots. Dick hasn't said anything yet, and the silence, the waiting, is almost worse than what will come. Tomorrow, on the hill, Mr. Gordon will fill the gopher holes with dirt and plant grass seed, but nothing will ever grow there.

At home, our mother's hands shake as she searches the phone book for Animal Control. After hanging up the phone, she lights a cigarette and stares at the toolbox, shushing our questions. Finally, she picks up the box and slides it into the freezer. We're supposed to freeze the gopher, she tells us, and then send it to Madison on Monday for rabies testing.

Rabies. Parents in our neighborhood have been talking about it ever since Beau the golden retriever had to be put to sleep after being bitten by a skunk. At the dinner table, my sister talks nonstop, stirring her SpaghettiOs with her bandaged hand, her spoon scraping and scraping against the blue plastic bowl. Since she can't have the gopher, she wants a guinea pig, or at least a gerbil. Maybe she already has rabies. Maybe at midnight she will leap from her bed, her teeth grown long and yellow, foam dripping from her mouth as she hovers in the closet connecting our bedrooms. I watch her for warning signs—excessive spit, red eyes, rapidly growing fingernails—as she does a word-search puzzle and watches *The Brady Bunch.*

There is no dessert, and we have to stay inside after supper. Our mother turns up the television to drown out the sounds of kids outside screaming and running in the thickening dusk, playing Bloody Murder. During commercials, my sister and I think up excuses to go to the kitchen, to open the freezer door and hear the gopher's nails against the toolbox. Each time, the air in the house seems thinner to me, more difficult to breathe. For hours, the gopher scrabbles back and forth in there. Then it stops.

MOTHS

How Funny

They step onto the porch, into the light of one bulb, and Daria feels it envelop her and Jeff, separate them from the night and the other people in it—the drab, serious people inside the houses along her street, who watch television in the dark, and the ones who pass by, shadows on the sidewalk in the washed-out dusk. Cicadas like rattlesnakes in the trees, and on the porch, in the spotlight, in Technicolor, Daria laughs up at Jeff, the man she will marry, even though she's not pregnant.

He likes her big laugh, she can tell. He likes that he has made it roll out of her. Mouth wide open.

That's when the little white moth enters, quick as a flash. Foolishly, she closes her lips, and it bumps against her tongue, her soft palate, her molars. It's all the things she never should have said flying back in, covering everything with a bitter dust. She spits it, raggedy, onto the flaking porch boards and then continues to laugh—high and strangled now with hilarity and shame—to convince both of them that she can laugh at herself.

It was the porch light that attracted it, of course. The light and her sweet, milky breath from the ice cream she's just eaten. Stupid to be standing under the porch light. Stupid to have just eaten the ice cream and then to go around with her mouth open.

Shut Your Mouth

She hears car tires and goes to the door again, one hand on top of her pregnant belly, one beneath, holding it like a football. The car passes without slowing, and the air hisses out of her lungs. Then she sees it hanging from the screen door: A moth like a miniature kite with green translucent wings, the two ends of its divided tail entwined like a ballerina's legs, tucked behind the ridiculously furred white body. Nature at its most indulgent. Nature playing a joke by etching on each wing the image of a heavy-lidded eye.

With difficulty, Daria crouches to examine it and then sits, staring into those eyes, and falls asleep propped against the wall, waking when the breeze shifts and comes through the screen suddenly cold. She opens her eyes, shivering, and finds two moths there now, moving together. They touch each other gently with legs the diameter of eyelashes, positioning, repositioning. She cannot stand to watch the care they take with one another. She closes the front door.

In a box in the basement, she finds the *Peterson First Guide to Butterflies and Moths*, many of its pages dog-eared. She bought it years ago to identify the moth that had flown into her mouth—probably a Corn Earworm Moth, *Helicoverpa zea*, but it was hard to tell from the mangled thing she'd finally spit out. She noticed moths after that, and butterflies, and looked them up in her book—Tiger, Leopard, Black Witch, Monarch, Skipper, Glassy-wing. For months, maybe even the entire first year she and Jeff were dating, whenever she saw one, she looked it up and folded down the page. It's a mystery, the book says, why moths are attracted to artificial light, perhaps because, as nocturnal creatures, they navigate by the light of the moon and are simply confused, their instincts stymied by civilization.

Daria can't remember when she put the book away in the basement to make room for another book on her shelf. Ten years have passed since she and Jeff met. She waited for the right time to have the baby, waited until they'd had their fun, waited to feel more sure of him, for him to grow up a little. Finally she got tired of waiting.

She finds an illustration of the moths on the door screen: Luna, *Actias luna*. Mating takes place after midnight. The female's scent attracts males across great distances—first-come, first-served. How must it feel, to come all that way, so certain? But the glory is short-lived: The book says the luna lives on larval fat just long enough to mate and lay eggs. Adult does not feed. Has no mouth in adult state. *Has no mouth. Does not feed.*

The words invoke a panic that makes Daria want to gorge, talk, kiss—but her reflex for fight or flight is faulty. When in danger, she freezes, plays dead to escape being mauled and eaten by predators. She finally manages to drag herself up the stairs to bed.

At three a.m., the buzz of the telephone on the pillow next to her catapults her from a dream of a fat green caterpillar baby she can't stop feeding, although she knows that feeding it will only facilitate the metamorphosis, after which she will be powerless to help her mouthless child.

Nature at Its Most Indulgent

Jeff is mostly unconscious—tanked, lit—when he leaves the bar, and he barely remembers getting into the car. He will never recall missing the curve or leaving the road. The car only makes a sound when it lands, nose-first in a hillock of field grass, sending up a flurry of white moths like confetti.

He has launched through the windshield and flipped completely, gracefully in the air before landing sprawled on his back on a sandy rise. Mere seconds later, another car approaches the scene. The driver slows, her passenger window down. She saw Jeff's car leave the road, and now there is no sound from the crash site. The male crickets in the field have been shocked into silence by the impact of the car, but as Marta idles there, she hears them click back on like an appliance. They start out tentatively, as if warming up, and then go all-out, competing for the only audience that matters.

She calls 911 from her cell phone, and then *hasta luego*. It's not that she doesn't recognize the car or the man—she was at the same bar, and she knows Jeff—or that she doesn't care. She just has to look out for *numero uno*.

When she sees him again, months later, his first night back at the bar, she doesn't tell him she was the one who called for help but didn't stop. Jeff is telling the story to the bartender, loud enough that all of them can hear, and as he talks, he rubs his thigh, probably the one he broke. Marta thinks it probably still itches where the cast came off, where the dead skin is probably still flaking away.

He flew from the car, he says, and landed on a hive of ground bees, who were drawn to the warmth of his body on that unseasonably cool night and so clustered around him, became attached to him—literally, figuratively. When the paramedics arrived and lifted him onto the stretcher, the bees defended their newfound territory. One of the EMTs was a history teacher he'd hated in high school. Now she was rescuing him, and in doing so, was stung so many times that she had a reaction and ended up in the hospital herself.

Jeff can tell that no one else thinks the story is as funny as he does; he's laughing way harder than anyone else. He looks sideways down the bar and sees that Marta is laughing but that her heart isn't really in it. When he told his wife, who was standing at the time with her pregnant belly pressed against the safety rail of his hospital bed, she didn't laugh at all.

He hasn't told anyone the other thing.

Number One

You're better off without her," Daria says.

She's leaning in the doorway of Miguel's office at the recreation center, where she works at the front desk and he works on the maintenance crew. She has curly black hair and a slender waist, around which she often wears a thick shiny belt. Miguel often wishes he could love her instead of his wife, wishes she could love him instead of her husband, who likes to drink and who yells too much at the solemn dark-eyed boy Miguel has watched grow up in photos on the bulletin board at Daria's desk. But Miguel knows he and Daria cannot love one another that way: they're too much alike. God has determined a role for every creature, and He has put Miguel and Daria on earth to do whatever they can for others, whenever they can, until there's nothing left.

Miguel's wife is gone again, and all day he prays that she's okay, praying still as he locks the rec center at the end of his shift and stands underneath the flickering light over the door, soon realizing that the flickering is caused not by a faulty bulb but by a moth that has somehow gotten trapped inside the light fixture.

There's a way out, Miguel tries to tell the moth. *It's the same way you got in*. He knows it is the moth's destiny to go to the light, but he cannot bear to watch its frantic orbit around the bulb, cannot bear the possibility that it will be burned to death by its own lack of perspective. He takes his keys from his pocket again. He'll just get the stepladder. But as he's turning back to the door, the flickering stops, and the moth is flying free into the night. Joy surges in Miguel's heart.

But in the next instant the joy is gone, and he is plunging even deeper into despair. *You again*, he thinks. *Hope—you bitch*.

He walks through a cloud of gnats to the curb, where he waits in the humid night for his cousin. Marta's taken the car this time and run off with her old boyfriend, an ex-con who appeared out of nowhere at their door last night. Marta opened the door, saw him standing there, and then just pulled her jean jacket from the back of the rocking chair, grabbed her shoes, and left without even putting them on, without a word.

Miguel has no tears left to cry. He rubs his swollen itching eyes with the heels of his hands. When he takes them away, something has appeared in the middle of the half-circle drive in front of the rec center, like a magic trick, something bright green against the black asphalt. He allows the little boy in him to become enchanted by it. He steps toward it. As in a fairy tale, perhaps a magical creature has come to grant him a wish. But he stops as he nears it, disturbed by its appearance—it is at least six inches long, with spiny legs like medical instruments. He remembers insect anatomy from grade school: they don't have noses or lungs but breathe through holes in their abdomens called *spiracles*. No wonder so many movie aliens look like bugs.

Surely his cousin will run over it when he pulls up. Miguel will pluck it from the drive and relocate it to one of the flower beds. He takes two more steps toward it, shaking off his discomfort. Its compound eyes are huge, iridescent. Is it watching him? He bends toward it, speaking softly, making a wish, just in case. *Te echo de menos, Marta. Wish you were here.* He swings his head side to side in what he hopes is a calming manner. *Ésta bien, bicho.* The mantis's eyes move side to side, too, tracking him.

Suddenly the bug springs straight at his face, and Miguel cries out and lifts his arms. He feels the mantis tap the back of his hand, and when he turns it over, it's still there, stuck to his skin with some sort of insect glue. He reaches to pull it off, but the instant he grasps the insect's body, it pinches the skin of his hand hard between its spiny forelegs, and Miguel cries out in pain and horror.

When Miguel's cousin arrives, Miguel is on his knees weeping next to a bed of zinnias where he has buried the mantis's body.

"*Vámonos,*" his cousin says, hauling him to his feet. He pats him hard on the back. "Let's go home."

As in a Fairy Tale

The boy crouches in the corner of the garage to get a better look. The spider is brown with elegant striped legs and an egg-shaped body many times the size of her head. She is busy wrapping a small colorless moth in gleaming thread.

The boy's mother has two stories about moths: Once upon a time, a moth flew into her mouth. She showed him how she'd looked when it happened, how she snapped her mouth closed and clapped her hand over it, and he laughed. Once upon another time, when he was still living inside her belly, she saw moths with eyes on their wings. She showed him pictures in a book, their bodies furry, their wings brilliant green.

His moth is duller, he knows, but they can look it up in the book, and the spider part of the story will make it worth telling. It's a large web, and there are several other insects suspended in it already, wrapped so thoroughly in white gossamer he can't tell what they were when they were alive. He blows on one part of the web, and everything in it ripples. The spider pauses in her work. Tanner's teacher said during science that maybe everything is connected this way, each person, each bug, each blade of grass sitting at a point in an invisible web that stretches to the ends of the universe. And when one thing on the web moves, the others feel it.

He notices that one of the wrapped orbs is shimmering, its edges soft. He leans closer and discovers that it's not food at all; the spider's egg sac has burst and is now teeming with minuscule transparent babies, some already casting webs and rappelling away. The flesh all over his body crawls. He felt the same way when his mother read him the library book that said millions of mites and bacteria live on the human body, even in his own mouth, under his fingernails, at the roots of his eyelashes. *We all need each other*, his mother said.

The door between the garage and the kitchen retracts with a sudden sucking sound, and Tanner flinches. His father's head appears. A good, warm smell comes out through the doorway.

"Boy, you want that three dollars or not?"

Tanner stands, nods mutely, but he knows it is already too late. He knew the second his father opened the door.

As if he hasn't answered at all, his father yanks the push broom from his hands and uses it to smash the spider web and its occupants, to sweep them out of the garage and into the driveway. Tanner wonders, his chest aching, how many of them are dead. The mother could be dead and it wouldn't matter, since the babies only need her until they hatch. Once they're out of the egg sac, they don't need their mother ever again. Then he thinks about how the mother spiders sometimes eat the fathers. There is some satisfaction in thinking she might have eaten him already.

Tanner watches his father move down the driveway with short, angry bursts of the broom. He's not going to give Tanner the three dollars, even though Tanner swept the entire floor, except for this corner. He could tell his mother, and she would stand up for him, but then the fight would be his fault.

He tries to comfort himself with a fact he read in a book: there are so many arthropods on Earth that people can't even count them. As his father mutters to himself in the driveway, brushing the spiders and debris into the gutter, Tanner imagines thousands of tiny spiders crawling up the handle of the broom, up his father's arms, covering his body as he screams like a little girl, something he's accused Tanner of doing. Tanner thinks of all the spiders in all the webs all over the world, how they multiply by the hundreds every minute, maybe even every second of the day.

Even a small patch of forest ground contains thousands of insects and arachnids. He imagines his father lying on the ground, surrounded by trees. He isn't wearing any clothes. His body shimmers, covered with spider babies and iridescent bees with transparent wings. From the layers of damp leaves beneath him, blue-black beetles emerge to crawl over his bare feet and along his hairy calves. Yet he does not move or even open his eyes, even when centipedes undulate over the webs between his fingers. Silver flies with spiky legs and red pinhead eyes alight on his lips, as though kissing him, and then fly away. When tiny yellow maggots appear at the corners of his mouth, as if by magic, Tanner knows they've come from the eggs the flies have laid there. He knows that flies lay their eggs on dead things so that when they hatch, the young will have something to eat. And he watches in his mind's eye with satisfaction as the insects writhe over his father's body until they have taken so many tiny bites taken from him that he disappears.

This could happen, Tanner thinks. His father could pay for what he's done, but his spirit could still go to Heaven, because God forgives everyone.

"What are you looking at?" his father asks, shoving the broom handle at Tanner as he walks by.

Piece of shit are the words that come into Tanner's mind. That's one of the things the decomposers eat: shit.

He hangs the broom on a nail that sticks out of the wall of the garage.

And then his mother's smiling face appears in the doorway, and he forgets his complaints about the three dollars, his sorrow for the spider and her babies, the image of his father disappearing little by little until there's nothing left.

"Come on, TJ," she says, in a way that almost always makes everything okay. "It's time to eat."

"I have to tell you something," he says breathlessly. "Spiders aren't even insects."

"They're not?"

He can tell she's pretending not to know, but he doesn't care.

"No, because all insects have six legs, and spiders have eight legs. They're arachnids."

She pretends to be surprised, too, and it makes him laugh as he walks past her into the kitchen. She follows him and turns on the water in the sink for him to wash his hands.

"And guess what?"

"What?"

"I saw a really big spider in the garage. A mother spider."

"I can't wait to hear about it."

As Tanner washes his hands, taking care to clean out under each one of his fingernails, he sees his father out of the corner of his eye, sitting at the table in front of his empty plate, his mouth twisted into the shape it takes when he's sure he's waited long enough.

His Body Shimmered

After Tanner was born, Jeff was so excited to have a boy, someone to watch baseball with, to go fishing with. But this boy belongs to Daria, lives for her, and it is always the two of them against him. This boy cried when Jeff tried to show him how to bait a hook with a worm. This boy thinks watching baseball is boring and wants to draw a picture of a spider instead. So Jeff watches the game alone while Tanner draws at the kitchen table.

Daria has gone out with her sister and left Jeff home with the boy, an unusual arrangement, and they are both uneasy as Tanner's bedtime approaches. Jeff orders the boy through the usual routine and then follows him down the hallway to his bedroom, tamping down a sense of panic.

Tanner climbs into his bed, pulls up the covers, and tucks his red stuffed dog, Jelly, into the crook of his arm. Jeff can tell he wants to suck his thumb, but he doesn't. Almost eight years old and still sucking his thumb! A hot wash of shame floods Jeff's body for calling him a thumb-sucking baby behind Daria's back.

Tanner, as though reading Jeff's thoughts, stares at him accusingly, his lips trembling as though he might cry. "I want Mom!" he says.

The words fly straight to Jeff's heart, a heart like a dartboard filled with all the sharp implements thrown so casually by his own son. Jeff sinks down onto the edge of the bed and tries to stroke the boy's tangled hair with a hand that feels too big and clumsy for the task. The gesture ends up more a facepalm than anything else, and Tanner jerks away from his touch.

"She'll be home soon," Jeff says in what he hopes is a soothing tone. He rises and turns toward the bookshelf. "How about if we read one of these books together? Isn't that what you and your mom do before you go to sleep?"

"Can you just tell me a story?" A hint of interest in the boy's voice now.

"Uh," Jeff says, feeling as though a football has hit him in the stomach. Telling stories is Daria's department. "I guess."

Tanner regards him as Jeff resettles himself on the edge of the bed.

"It was very dark, driving out there in the middle of nowhere," he begins.

"You forgot 'Once upon a time,'" Tanner offers matter-of-factly.

"Oh, yeah," Jeff says, trying not to laugh. "Once upon a time, before you were born, I was driving down a dark, dark road in the middle of nowhere."

Tanner nods approvingly.

"It was so dark that I missed a curve in the road, and my car went flying into a field. I flew out of the car through the windshield, and when I landed on my back, it was right on top of a hive of bees—special bees that live in the ground."

"Bees live in the ground?" Tanner says.

"Some of them do," Jeff says, nodding. He can tell that Tanner is holding back his many questions about the bees. He can feel Tanner wanting him to keep talking.

"I was technically unconscious, lying there in the dark, on top of the beehive, but I remember it, sort of like a dream." Jeff tries to stop his voice from shaking. He's never told anyone this part, not even Daria. "I felt suspended in a dark place, and then I started to feel a tingling in my back, here—" He indicates the small of his back. "And then that tingling, buzzing feeling began to crawl down my legs to my feet, to my toes, and up my back to my arms and all the way to my fingers, and up my neck and up over my head to the middle of my forehead. And I was all lit up in the darkness like a network of wire and lightbulbs, like a science experiment."

"Was it the bees lighting you up?" Tanner whispers.

Jeff shakes his head. "I don't know. But when they came to take me to the hospital—"

"Who came to take you?"

"The EMTs, the people in the ambulance."

"What happened to you?"

"I broke my leg." He rubs his left thigh unconsciously. "Got a concussion."

Tanner nods gravely. "What happened when they took you?"

"I was all lit up, like I said, and when they lifted me off the beehive, the lights went out as though they had pulled a plug." As he says it, he struggles not to cry. The sense of loss he felt then is still so strong.

"One of the EMTs told me later that the bees were attracted to the warmth of my body, and when the people who were trying to help me lifted me up off the ground, the bees got mad and started stinging them."

"But they didn't sting you."

"Not once."

"They wanted you to stay."

"I guess so."

Since the last time Jeff told the story, years ago, it has changed. It's not really funny anymore. Tanner's hand creeps into Jeff's where it lies on the bed, and Jeff clasps it gently.

"Can we get a book from the library about the bees that live in the ground?" Tanner says.

"I think so," Jeff says.

Tanner yawns. "Then I can draw a picture of you all lit up by bees," he says.

"Sure," Jeff says. He lies down on the pillow next to his boy as he's seen Daria do, just to keep him company until he falls asleep.

THE PEARL OF HIM

She finds him sitting alone at the window in his room. The midmorning sun shines through the pale spray of his hair, lighting in agonizing detail the crusted trace of milk down the front of his Henley, the dried flake of cereal glued there like a misshapen extra button.

She should never have brought him here. But where, then?

She is surprised to see a book open across his lap, because he has seemed unable to read for a long time. But his eyes scan the print, and his mouth moves, and he begins to claw at the page, as though to dig a hole through the words. As she recognizes the gilt-edged pages, the black leatherette cover, her heart stutters, and the sensation makes her cough.

"Where on earth did you get that?" she manages. But he doesn't answer.

His memories have receded, scuttled away like the untouchable ghost crabs they chased so gleefully when they lived on Chesapeake Bay when they were first married and worked at the Country Day School. They were night birds then, could get by on so little sleep in the summertime. They watched the schedule to know when to safely build a fire on the beach. Now something else is surging to overtake them both, her own rageful sorrow like a swift and terrifying dark tide.

It hasn't occurred to her until now that the bedrock of his beliefs—his faith in rationality above all, the atheism he has worn like a badge of honor and defiance since he was a teenage socialist—could crumble without disintegrating his flesh and bone. Now that he is trapped in those secret places, out of her reach, has he learned something he didn't know before? She wants to believe that the pearl of him is still in there, though his mind is closed so tightly against her now, the silence between them loud in her ears, the ocean in a shell.

And who has given him a damned Bible? Which of the young underpaid nonunion workers? They sag bonelessly against the counter, staring at their phones. They cannot be bothered to clean him up after meals or even when he's wet through to his trousers. They have to be asked to do the smallest thing, which she then has to pay for as though it's a personal favor. Or did he seek the book out, pick it up off a shelf or table?

"Have you been reading that, then?" she asks, terrified of the answer.

He looks at her for a long moment, craning forward in his chair, lifting a trembling hand toward her. Finally, he nods.

"Do you believe it?" she asks.

His eyes flash almost-green, a storm over the Atlantic. One side of his mouth lifts in the old wry smile, and he says, "This shit? Never."

PARADISE IS A PLACE WITH PLENTY OF MUSIC

John likes to eat his Cheerios on the sun porch, even when there's no sun. Monday morning, a Vivaldi concerto plays on the radio, its violins describing the wind outside that bends the trees in the backyard like archery bows. John spoons cereal into his mouth and scans the *Wall Street Journal*. The former Soviet Union is lurching toward capitalism; Castro calls Western democracy "complete garbage"; Saddam Hussein remains defiant in the face of sanctions. Despite lowered interest rates, the real-estate market continues to stagnate. IBM is in trouble, and a man in Boston claims to have been poisoned by a combination of lawn pesticides and Tagamet. But these issues cannot compete with Clarence Thomas and Anita Hill, whose story John is tired of hearing about, though certainly every person he talks to today will mention it.

It is all over the front page, above the fold: "The Thomas Hearings—Unsolved Mysteries: Even If Confirmed, Judge Thomas Will Be Under Cloud of Doubt—Senate Hearings Fail to Prove That He or Prof. Anita Hill Is the More

Believable—The Showdown on Tuesday."The Vivaldi violins seem to grow shriller as he reads what might as well be on the cover of *People* or *Parade*: "Behind the scenes, Judge Thomas's supporters and friends repeatedly muttered phrases such as '*Fatal Attraction* syndrome,' alluding to a movie about spurned love and revenge, in an effort to paint Ms. Hill as a sociopath." The front-page editorial mixes metaphors, comparing Thomas to the lone protester in Tiananmen Square, the Senate Democrats to a lynch mob.

This past weekend, if Georgia wasn't watching the confirmation hearing itself, she managed to find some commentary about it on television, talking heads who continued talking when there was nothing more to say. John had to bribe her with dinner at the Blue Marlin to even get her out of the house.

He is clearing his breakfast dishes from the table on the sun porch when his neighbor Steve appears in the driveway next door and gets into his Volkswagen. Steve can't park in his garage because Lynette, his wife, has claimed one side of it for her car and filled the other with boxes of summer clothes, old papers, and discarded exercise equipment. Steve has a permanent hangdog look, which John has noticed in many married men, as though he'd happily set out to marry a bossy woman without understanding the long-term consequences. John prides himself on having maintained most of the opinions he had before he met Georgia, including his suspicion that marriage brings out the worst in both parties. The subject has only come up between them as a joke.

In the kitchen, he shoves the newspaper deep into the garbage can and washes his dishes at the sink, noting with mild shock that Georgia has washed her juice glass and wiped her toast crumbs from the counter, though probably only onto the floor. On his way to the bathroom he can hear her humming something, and he pauses to listen in the hall outside their bedroom. What is that tune? Undetected, he watches Georgia comb her hair and smooth lotion on her arms and legs in front of the mirror, the slight bend of her body reminding him of Botticelli's Venus, newly born and riding the oyster shell to shore, her hair curling against the rose-pink of her skin, the light of the lamp reflected in the mirror like white waves.

He waits there, lulled by the sound of her voice. There are moments like this when Georgia's presence in his house seems as ordinary as his own, times when her shoes lined up in the entryway seem perfectly natural, times when it doesn't startle him to close the bathroom door and find her pale silky robe hanging there like the skin of an animal.

The name of the song occurs to him then: "You Don't Know What Love Is." Chet Baker, from the album they listened to last night.

It's true that his guts twist a little each time he walks into the bedroom they've shared now for more than a year, a room rendered substantially smaller by Georgia's mammoth dresser and the mound of clothing draped over the back of the armchair.

It had happened without warning one May evening, after Georgia mentioned that the lease on her apartment would soon expire. The two of them were in John's bed, but it was still light outside, and the evening sun drew bright lines around the blinds. Georgia was hunting for her bra and underwear among the sheets, wearing only a pair of thin white ankle socks, and John was contemplating the perfect trough of her spine.

Since meeting her, he had begun to see his earlier experiences with women as casual, his sexual interest and their halfhearted pretense at pleasure as silly compared to the intensity of his desire now and the sound of Georgia's voice climbing the scale like a hoarse clarinet. Her voice had captivated him the instant he'd heard it.

Georgia finally found her bra between the pillows. "So anyway," she said, arranging it on John's chest so that the beige cups covered his nipples, "I'm looking at a place on Spaight Street tomorrow after school. Should I just come over here afterward?" Her fingernails were painted bright pink with white polka dots. Within that context, John's question seemed perfectly logical.

"Why don't you just move in here?" he asked.

Georgia leaned back on her heels and scanned his face with her brown almond-shaped eyes. John kept very still. It wasn't the first time she'd searched his face for something, nor the first time he'd wondered whether she would find it.

"What's the matter?" he asked.

"I'm afraid!" Georgia said. "Aren't you afraid?"

John laughed. He was fairly certain he hadn't been truly afraid since he was a child. And Georgia made him feel giddy, brave, foolhardy.

"No," he answered, grinning. "What are you afraid of?"

"Well, now I'm afraid because you're not afraid."

John reached out and traced the bumps of her larynx. Often when she spoke, he longed to be immersed in the reedy sound of it or to enter it like a room and close the door.

"I want this," he said, and he kissed her.

Georgia pulled away, frowning. "You have to know it's not going to be like this all the time. We'll fight, you'll grow to resent me . . . and then we'll have to get married."

They laughed for a long time, and John felt buoyant and happy. Then Georgia wiped the tears from beneath her eyes and said, "Okay, then."

And when John woke the next morning with her ankle-bone resting painfully on his instep, and when he noticed the trail of clothes leading from the chair to her side of the bed, panic soured his stomach. What impulse had led him to ask such a question without considering its ramifications? Hadn't the current arrangement been working perfectly for him? My God, they hadn't even known each other six months! He was nearly overwhelmed in that moment by the urge to disentangle himself. As he contemplated his future, John thought it might be wise to make a clean break, to never see Georgia again, to return to the kind of anonymous coupling that didn't even entail staying the night.

Then Georgia, still half-asleep, rolled toward him. A wayward curl of her hair tickled his nose. Her hand disappeared beneath the blanket and found his bare hip. She kissed him lightly on the mouth, once, twice, and the urge to break it off faded, though it seems never to have left him completely. He can feel it rising inside him from time to time, like a genie in a bottle—this Monday morning, for instance, when he lifts the toilet lid and finds a horrific mess in the bowl. He steps back, and the lid falls with a loud clatter.

Georgia knows the story of how, as a boy, John threw back the toilet lid one afternoon and came face to face with a bloody unflushed mass, a white string snaking out from it like the fuse on a stick of dynamite. His brother Robert had shit his guts out! Or someone had murdered their mother and thrown her eviscerated organs into the toilet! The killers might still be in the house. He had to get out—fast. He darted down the hallway and, rounding the corner into the kitchen, ran squarely into his mother, who clutched at him to keep her balance, inadvertently pressing his face into her breasts.

John's mother sat him down that morning and explained in gory detail the fate of all women. As she spoke, a dirty smell like the ground after rain seeped from under her clothing and forced its way into John's nostrils.

"Georgia!" he yells now.

"Are you okay?" she calls, and then she is there in the bathroom doorway, wearing only her underwear. "What's wrong?"

From the corner farthest from the toilet, he points mutely.

"What?" She slides past him and lifts the toilet lid, and then she lets it fall again. "I'm sorry, John," she says, rolling her eyes. "I forgot to flush. You couldn't just flush it yourself?"

He tries to ignore the way the lacy bra holds her breasts out to him.

"You could have warned me."

"Warned you about what?"

Her thin lips almost disappear when she's angry, and her voice reminds him of a viola, the bow drawn roughly across the strings.

"Do you want me to wear a sign around my neck? Should I embroider a scarlet *P* on my clothing so you don't accidentally touch me and soil yourself? I forgot that you're from that fairy-tale land where women don't bleed. Did they send you here to study us dirty people?"

Once she gets started, she goes on and on. So what if John doesn't like to make love during that time of the month? He's explained that it's simply a preference, something he can't change, but she insists it's *sexist*.

She turns away and abruptly leaves the bathroom.

"Aren't you going to flush it?" he asks.

"No, I'm not," she calls.

"It doesn't matter that it's nauseating to me? That I might even throw up if I have to do it?"

"You're a big boy, John. You take care of it. I'm already late for dress rehearsal."

The elementary school where she teaches music is putting on a Peanuts Halloween program.

It's a bad beginning to what turns out to be a crummy day. Ninety minutes later, John makes excruciating small talk with a new client, Peter Solis, while the two of them wait for John's assistant, Katherine, to locate the materials she was supposed to prepare for the appointment.

Katherine graduated from the university in the spring with a bachelor's degree in marketing, and though she's creative and intelligent, she's not the most organized assistant John's ever had. He would never admit that, during her interview, he was captivated most not by her credentials but by the contrast between her long white neck and her deep red hair, the way she swept her bangs out of her eyes with a graceful white hand. This is the third embarrassing mistake she's made in the few months since John hired her, and he realizes grimly that he will have to fire her. She has made him look unprofessional for the last time.

Mr. Solis is a paunchy man in dark high-water trousers and white socks who has asked the firm to market his line of multicultural puppets. John pours him a cup of coffee from the pot in the corner of his office and then sits down and smiles across the desk at him, trying not to watch Katherine flit back and forth beyond the doorway.

"Have you been watching the hearings?" Solis asks.

John tries not to sneer. "A little bit, yes."

"She seems like she's got a screw loose, don't you think? Those quiet types, you never know when they're going to just crack and go crazy on you."

John nods noncommittally. It really isn't the time or place to air his opinions on Anita Hill. He glances at his client's stubby hands dangling from the armrests of his chair. On one, a huge class ring with a red stone; on the other, a thick gold wedding band.

"You must be married to an extrovert," John says.

Solis laughs atonally and then launches into a description of his lovely wife, who has done all the sewing on the puppet prototypes.

"What about you, John? Are you married?" Solis asks.

"No, I'm single," John says. He smiles genuinely for the first time today but feels his irritation surge anew when he realizes he's smiling because he knows how Georgia would laugh if she heard him tell such a lie.

After lunch, Katherine slinks into his office, grimacing, and John thinks of the way the Irish setter puppy he had as a boy used to approach their cranky old spaniel.

"I am so sorry, John," Katherine says. "I don't know what happened."

It must be unconscious the way her hands flutter at chest level, drawing his eyes to her full breasts. She is wearing a forest-green wraparound dress that plunges in front and ties at one side of her small waist. An hourglass figure.

"I thought I had put all the materials on the cart, but I had accidentally filed one folder away. It was really stupid—"

"Katherine," he interrupts. "Don't worry about it." He can't believe he's saying it even as his lips are forming the words. "Solis signed the contract at lunch," he says, and one side of his mouth lifts involuntarily.

"Really?" Katherine says, wide-eyed. "That's great news!"

She smiles, and the unabashed relief on her face sends a jolt through him.

"So," he says, leaning back in his chair, "let's go have a beer after work to celebrate."

It isn't unusual for the people in John's office to socialize after hours, and he isn't eager to run home and finish the argument he and Georgia started this morning. Katherine's eyes shift toward the windows behind his desk.

"I'm sorry," she says, "I have plans for dinner."

Her eyes swing back to his, and he can't tell if she really is sorry or if she's just being polite. John wants to laugh. Does she think he's asking her on a date? She knows he and Georgia live together, and if he remembers correctly, Katherine has mentioned a boyfriend. But what do Georgia and Katherine's boyfriend have to do with getting a beer? Women take everything so seriously.

When John gets home, Georgia is sitting on the couch, her eyes glued to PBS, which is rebroadcasting the last day of testimony for viewers whose stamina gave out before the hearing ended at two a.m. There are white cartons on the coffee table from their favorite Thai restaurant—an apology? Georgia waves John over to the couch, puts her arm around his shoulders, and kisses his cheek—all without taking her eyes from the television screen—as though the gesture is supposed to make up for the fact that she had a hand in ruining his day.

"This John Doggett's a real piece of work," she says. "They're supposed to tell briefly who they are, but instead he brags for fifteen minutes about how *Nightline* and *Good Morning America* want to interview him. Now Biden's ripping him to pieces."

The witness is an unattractive Black man with a bad hairline who raises his eyebrows as Senator Biden speaks.

"She may not be telling the truth," Biden says, "but how one can draw the conclusion from that kind of exchange that this is a woman who is fantasizing, this is a woman who must have a problem because she has turned— Are you a psychiatrist?"

"Senator," Doggett says, "I am trying to follow your question, but I may have to ask you to restate it."

"My question is," Senator Biden bellows, "are you a psychiatrist?"

"Absolutely not."

"Are you a psychologist?"

"Absolutely not."

The senator leans in and clutches the microphone, as though he is about to climb over the table and challenge the witness to a wrestling match.

"Well," he says, "how, from that kind of an exchange, can you draw the conclusion that she obviously has a serious problem, that she—Where is the section? I want to find it here in your statement. You were stunned by her statement. You told her her comments were totally uncalled for and completely unfounded. Balderdash!"

Georgia laughs delightedly, a gorgeous sound like a scale played on a glockenspiel, and the pleasure it evokes in John only adds to his irritation. She hasn't even apologized.

"I can't wait for Angela Wright's and Sukari Hardnett's testimony," Georgia says. "Do you know when they were on? Was it right at the end?"

"They decided not to testify," John says.

"What?"

"That's all I know, that they didn't testify."

"I can't believe it. What happened?"

"I have no idea."

He wonders how Georgia thinks a congressional committee can make sense of what happened between two people in private ten years ago. What makes her think there is any sense to be made of it in the first place? They could talk for months and never get to the bottom of it. Besides, John hates Joe Biden and his blond comb-over. Talk about a showboat.

"Did she come up to you and say, in mildly hysterical terms, 'Why have you not called me?'" Biden asks. "Or did she just make the statement straight, monotone, 'You shouldn't lead somebody on like that,' or whatever the precise statement was?"

"God," John says, raising a hand in front of his eyes, "this is painful. Can't you just read about it in the paper?"

"You don't have to watch it," Georgia says, scooping green curry and rice into her mouth. Some of the rice escapes her fork and scurries like bugs into the cracks between the sofa cushions.

John puts a load of laundry into the washer and then eats curry and rice in the armchair near the baby grand—the chair where he usually sits when Georgia plays—with the stereo headphones clamped over his ears. Haydn's Symphony No. 96, "Miracle," the Pannon Philharmonic, drowns out the television. Each time he comes back to this symphony, it is the same. If another orchestra played it, he would recognize it. And while he might notice something new each time he listens to this particular recording—the dialogue here in the first movement between the brass and the woodwind, for instance—the new details only serve to make the piece more layered, more complex. The surprise will never be an unpleasant one. It's different with people. Their loyalties shift; they change their minds. You can't learn a person like a song.

Later, getting into bed, John asks, "Are we enemies?"

"Oh, John, no!" Georgia lets *Time* magazine drop over the edge of the bed onto the floor, where it will become bent and wrinkled before he has a chance to read it. She lies down next to him on his pillow, too close.

"Then why do you attack me when I do or say something you disagree with?"

Georgia sighs and flops back onto her own side of the bed. "It's not just that I disagree. It's that you're . . . well, you're wrong. Don't you want to keep growing? Don't you want to be a better person?"

"So I'm supposed to change whatever it is about me you think is wrong?"

"This is about behavior, John."

"Exactly. But it's about *my* behavior, right? You don't have to change your behavior, but I have to change mine."

John feels the adrenaline pour into his bloodstream, preparing him for the inevitable escalation. But Georgia only slumps back against the headboard. "Touché," she says through pursed lips.

"You know," John says, glancing at the book on his night-stand, unable to stop himself, though he knows she might laugh, "one of the seven habits of highly effective people is 'First try to understand others, then try to be understood.'"

Georgia nods. She takes his hand and squeezes it. He can't remember the last time he's had the last word.

As she turns onto her side and pulls the blanket up over her shoulder, John says, "Hey, I have to take my car to the mechanic in Shorewood tomorrow after work. The exhaust is really loud, but the muffler looks fine. Steve thinks it might be the manifold. Anyway, could you come and pick me up at the garage about six?"

"Of course."

After Georgia closes her eyes, John tries to read but only ends up staring at her face. The first time he saw her was at the symphony orchestra. He was in the lobby of the civic center sipping wine with his brother, Robert, and Robert's wife, Nancy. John's program slipped from his fingers, and as he bent to pick it up, he bumped backsides with Georgia, who was standing behind him and who just happened to bend down at that same moment—to brush a drop of wine from her leather boot, she told him later. It was a perfect slapstick moment, but John isn't a fan of slapstick. His face was hot with annoyance as he turned to face Georgia, who was laughing.

"Excuse me! I am so sorry," she said, laying her hand on his arm, and he stared at her, unable to process the low flute of her voice, her slight overbite. She was wearing a deep red turtleneck and matching lipstick.

"That's okay," he said and then stared dumbly at her mouth, hoping she would speak again, that he would be able to think of something that would make her laugh.

Nancy turned toward John and Georgia just then.

"Georgia!" she said. The two women hugged, and Nancy introduced her as the music teacher at Randall Elementary School, where Nancy worked as a nurse.

"You have a very distinctive voice," John said, feeling a blush run up his neck the moment the words left his mouth. As if she'd never heard that one before.

Georgia laughed, and the sound, like the snap of a hypnotist's fingers, made him forget how foolish he'd felt.

"Thanks, I think," she said. "You have very distinctive sideburns."

The blush began to burn again in his cheeks and forehead. He had been shaving his sideburns a little longer lately, emulating recent pictures in *GQ*. How long had it been since a girl had made him blush?

The chimes rang, indicating the end of intermission, but John was distracted during the rest of the concert and even at work the next day. On his way home, against his better judgment, against his will, he stopped by Robert and Nancy's house to see if Nancy had Georgia's phone number, even though she really didn't seem like his type.

"She thinks you're gorgeous," Nancy said as she paged through her address book.

"She does?"

Women usually responded positively to John, so why was it so difficult for him to believe that Georgia would find him attractive? Why did he feel so stunningly inept?

"I told her how uptight you are, but she didn't seem to mind," Nancy said. "God, John, I'm just kidding. Stop looking at me like that."

"Christ, John, relax," Robert said from the recliner, where he was drinking a bottle of beer.

It was a refrain Robert had been repeating since the two of them were boys, and John wished he could simply comply, just decide to take life a little less seriously.

Initially, Georgia's presence did seem to relax him. John lay on the sofa in her small apartment, dazed as she played Chopin concertos on her old upright piano or sang "Spring Can Really Hang You Up the Most" over rippling chords. He wanted to know everything about her. He wanted to buy her a baby grand.

But lately the steady pressure of her influence seems to threaten his very identity. Does she want him to be a man who will cater to her every whim, pick up after her, have sex with her when he finds the idea repugnant? And what of the reserve, the stability and business sense she said had attracted her to him in the first place? Would she throw those characteristics out the window, the baby with the bathwater? He suspects that she has misrepresented herself, that she has pretended since the beginning to be satisfied with who he is.

Now she lies on her side next to him with one hand folded beneath her chin. There are lines etched from the corners of her mouth, corkscrew curls pointing various directions. The woman he met that night at the symphony wore her hair pulled back in a smooth twist, allowing a silhouette of her straight nose and strong rounded chin. A woman whose heart melted for the strains of Vivaldi violins.

How can the same woman find it funny to imitate Beavis and Butthead when John happens to say the word "head" or mentions his colleague Dick? Just last week, while they were getting ready for bed, she ground her pelvis against John's thigh and sang "I Wanna Sex You Up" with a mouthful of toothpaste. And when he frowned down at her, she only laughed harder.

John turns off his lamp and settles onto his back. Then he hears it rising in the dark, the delicate, nearly inaudible snore.

ON TUESDAY NIGHT, John waits nearly thirty minutes before Georgia finally pulls into the minuscule parking lot of the garage. For God's sake! He just reminded her that morning!

He jerks open the passenger door to find Georgia sobbing behind the wheel. Her face is wet and blotchy. The car reeks of cigarettes. When did she start smoking again? And what on earth is the matter? He recalls a similarly emotional scene a few weeks ago, when Dr. Seuss died.

"What's wrong?" he asks, unsuccessfully trying to keep the irritation out of his voice. "Do you want me to drive?"

She shakes her head, and he reluctantly gets into the passenger seat.

"Didn't you hear?" she says in a voice thick and throaty as a French horn. "They confirmed the bastard."

John barely has a chance to pull his door closed before she forces the long car into a U-turn, her right front bumper nearly hitting a parked car.

"You're crying because they confirmed Clarence Thomas?" John settles his briefcase between his knees and fastens his seatbelt. Then he notices Georgia is glaring at him through her tears.

"Sorry," he says, wishing she would watch the road. "I'm just surprised. You weren't expecting it?"

"How could they put such a person on the Supreme Court?"

How can she be so naive? Should he explain to her that the confirmation hearings are little more than a formality, that unless the candidate has been killing and eating kittens and babies, he is guaranteed the rubber stamp? It's all just a show, a carnival that even the *Wall Street Journal* has fallen all over itself to attend. John clutches the door handle as Georgia squeals around a corner on a yellow light. One day she'll kill them both.

"What a colossal waste of time," he mutters. "I hope it was worth it for Anita Hill."

"What?" Georgia brakes too late at a traffic signal, and John slides toward the dashboard.

"Could you please slow down?" he asks. "I said I hope it was worth the money Kennedy's minions paid Anita Hill."

"You think she's lying?"

"Maybe they had a little office flirtation or something. It's possible. But maybe they didn't." John loosens his tie. "Maybe he said a few things at work that offended her. My guess is she either made it up or exaggerated the situation."

"Of course." Georgia's voice moves into her throat again. There was a time when they were first dating when she would read part of the local newspaper aloud to him each evening after supper. When had she stopped doing that?

"You can be a real asshole, John," she says.

"What did I do?"

"Why do you automatically think she's lying? He's the one who's lying, by the way. He has all the reason in the world to lie. She doesn't. His testimony was so over the top—"

"I read his testimony, and I thought it was quite convincing."

The traffic light changes, and Georgia stomps down on the gas.

"You heard what John Doggett said about her going-away party," John continues. "She cornered him and accused him of leading her on when he'd never had the slightest interest in her in the first place."

Georgia scoffs, "If anyone was getting paid, it was him. Hell, they probably didn't even have to pay him to get up there and make a fool of himself." She wipes her nose on the back of her hand.

"What about the other women who testified on his behalf?" John asks. "Maybe she doesn't even know she's making it up. Maybe she's one of those women who thinks every man she comes in contact with wants her. 'Oh, he looked at me wrong. Oh, he told a dirty joke. Oh, I just got a bad feeling when he was around.'"

"And they're all lying."

"I said exaggerating."

"Okay, well what about Angela Wright? What happened to her? Who silenced her?"

"I'm sure she got cold feet after hearing those other women testify. Anita Hill worked for the EEOC, for God's sake. Are you telling me she didn't know the proper procedure for filing a sexual harassment claim?"

"Men do this to women *every day*," Georgia says. "And then they blame the victim, as a warning to the rest of us. This is standard operating procedure. Are you really this blind? I can't even talk to you about this anymore."

John can't feel sorry about her declaration. He has imagined paradise more than once as a place with little talking. He is tired of the constant negotiations that come with language, that thicket of thorns. Give him a symphony: resolution in three movements.

At home, they eat in silence. When John joins Georgia in bed, her eyes are closed, though he knows she's not asleep.

"I need to ride with you tomorrow," he says to her back.

She says nothing.

At seven thirty the next morning, John gets into Georgia's station wagon and waits there fifteen minutes before she comes out of the house. She doesn't even say goodbye when he gets out of the car outside his office building.

At noon, John calls the garage and learns his car won't be ready until Thursday. He leaves a message on the answering machine at home asking Georgia to pick him up at five thirty, but she never returns his call. At five forty, he swivels in his chair toward the windows and scans the street outside half-heartedly for her car, and then he picks up the phone and punches in their number again, wondering how he has come to depend on someone so completely unreliable.

As the phone rings at home, John watches the elms that line the street outside disrobe in the thinning daylight, flooding the gutters with deep red leaves. The answering machine finally picks up, and John listens to Georgia's voice saying, "John and Georgia can't come to the phone right now, but please leave a—" He slams the receiver down just as Katherine pokes her head into his office. She flinches.

"I was going to ask if you need me to do anything before I take off," she says, "but is everything okay?"

John smiles wanly. "I'm not having such a good afternoon."

"I'm sorry." Katherine tips her head to the side and her hair shifts, a burgundy curtain.

"Georgia and I are arguing," John says, though he can't imagine why he is telling her such a thing. "We've been doing that a lot lately."

He knows he should stop talking, but there's something urging him forward, the suggestion of intimacy, however false or fleeting. He just wants to feel better.

"You know how when you first fall in love with someone, you love every little thing about them—the way they brush their teeth, the way they tie their shoes or leave their shoelaces flapping, as the case may be."

Katherine's laugh is a tinkling insubstantial sound.

"Then it's as though you're sobering up after being drunk, and everything looks different."

John thinks Katherine probably has no idea what he's talking about. How much experience can she possibly have? She's twenty-two years old, barely graduated from college. He rubs his face with both hands. She stares at him, her lips parted slightly.

"If I've been especially hard to work with this last month or so," he says, "I apologize."

"Oh, God, no," Katherine says. "I should be apologizing to you. I'm sure I made your life even more difficult by screwing up the Solis account—"

"Come on, forget about that," John says, though not a day has passed since then that he hasn't thought about firing her. "Anyway, sorry for the outburst. Thanks for listening. Oh, could you, before you go, take a look at this fax you gave me earlier? A couple of the lines are smeared. Maybe you can decipher them."

Katherine walks around to John's side of the desk and leans over the paper. Her shoulder is only inches from his face, her hair fallen down between them, the skin on her neck and forearms luminous. He's never seen such skin on a girl.

"Hmm," she says, bending closer to the desktop.

"What does it say right there?" John asks, leaning in and pointing to the blurred line. There is a vibration in the air between them. Katherine turns slightly to look at him. Her eyes are sherry brown with darker brown starbursts around the irises, and they are open wide—with what? Anticipation? Surprise? John reaches up and touches her face with his thumb, just to the right of her mouth.

"You've got a little pen mark right there," he says. Then he smiles.

"Oh." Katherine straightens from the desk and her hand goes to her cheek, which is now bright pink. "Oh, thanks. I—I—can't make out those lines, either. I'll—just—call in the morning and have them send it through again. Sorry about that."

When she reaches the threshold, John says, "Goodnight, Katherine." His words contain an invitation—to what, exactly, John isn't certain, but he knows he does not want to go home just yet, knows he does not want to sit in his brother's living room and endure Robert's meaningless advice—but if Katherine hears it, she doesn't acknowledge it, only waves over her shoulder without looking back.

"See you tomorrow, John."

He calls a taxi to take him home and watches from the window as the trees rush by. The locusts are already bare, their branches black as ink. The maples go in patches, red against the green like a head wound, like an infrared photo of the body's warmth. He gets out of the car and walks up the driveway through a river of leaves. This time of year always smells of burning; white clouds stretch across the darkening sky, skeletons of fish with the flesh burned away.

He is startled to find Georgia's car missing from its usual place at the curb, and worry bumps up against his annoyance.

The *Capital Times* is still lying at the edge of the driveway. Has something happened to her? John scoops up the paper and hurries inside, where the light on the answering machine is blinking with his own undelivered message. There is a note on the dining room table.

Dear John, it begins, and he thinks that perhaps Georgia has left him. Would she really leave him over this? His heart beats painfully hard, his surprise hurting him physically. It's funny how he has never considered that she would leave him. He has always pictured the end of their relationship as his own doing. *I'm spending a day or two at my mom's to think things through. I'll call you. Georgia*

What does it mean? John pushes the question away, focusing instead on action. He will drive to Georgia's mother's house right now and insist that they talk about it. Maybe he has been too harsh, insensitive even. He hears Georgia's voice saying, *Are you really this blind?* Would he have said those things about Anita Hill if he hadn't been so angry at Georgia?

He will go to her mother's house and insist on seeing her. But first he should eat something. He goes to the cupboard and finds a can of tomato soup, and as he pours it into the pan, he remembers how, through Georgia, he discovered certain small spontaneities in himself he hadn't known existed. In the beginning, he would be on his way somewhere—to the grocery store or to meet friends at a bar—and he would end up instead on her doorstep. When she opened the door and found him there, a light appeared in her eyes.

"Oh, it's you," she said soberly one night as he stood on the threshold, and then she laughed, and he walked into that sound and closed the door.

But she probably doesn't want him coming to her mother's house tonight without calling first. He'll try to call her later. Maybe he'll call his brother. Maybe Nancy will know what he should do.

As the soup warms, John grills a cheese sandwich and then takes his meal and the newspaper to the porch. Next door, Steve and Lynette are working on their yard, as they often do in the evenings, and the light from the fixture mounted on their garage spills into the room and across the table where John sits. He is distracted by a pressure in the periphery of his mind, like a tide that seems to have the potential to drown him. He refuses to turn toward it, to look at it head-on.

He turns on the radio. The sound of a flute floats out and narrates the shadows, the shush of wind outside. He forces himself to concentrate on the high sweet sound of it, on the warm salty soup, on the evening headlines, on the image of Katherine's hair falling across her white neck.

Georgia's temper will cool, and she'll come home, and they will come to some agreement about Anita Hill and Clarence Thomas—perhaps only that the topic, like capital punishment, belongs on the list of things they can't discuss without arguing. Afterward, they will fall together on the bed, the light from the hallway gilding Georgia's skin.

He will not allow himself to consider the other possibilities. He will not consider the meaning of his own ambivalence of the past months. He will not think about the film of tears illuminating Georgia's eyes last night as they ate in silence or the way her body hunched toward the steering wheel this morning as though she were struggling under a great weight, as though John's presence in the passenger seat made her smaller. He refuses to believe that the bright insistence in her has dimmed.

He redirects his thoughts to how much he likes the sound of the flute floating out of the radio and the taste of tomato soup with a grilled cheese sandwich. He thinks about how he should buy stock in a cellular phone company.

He stares out the window at his neighbor Steve, who is up on a ladder pounding nails into the back porch. He's been working on it since the beginning of summer, yet it's still little more than a frame, bare greenish ribs where the roof should be.

A SCUBA LESSON

Hilda had known Gregory ten years before she called him on it. It took her that long to get over her first impression—that Gregory was a jackass—and her second impression—that Gregory was an unhappy jackass—and to arrive at her third impression—that underneath, Gregory was a pretty nice guy, as far as guys go.

One night at the local tap, he said it again for the benefit of a new instructor: "I can teach any turkey to scuba dive!"

Hilda waved to him across the table. "I have turkeys," she said.

"What?" One gin and tonic and he had cute red patches—like rug burn—low on his cheeks.

She smiled broadly. "I bet you can't teach one of my turkeys to dive."

The scuba crowd cheered.

She was still married then to her first husband, a hobby farmer who owned the shop where Gregory's students rented equipment. Years later, her feet in Gregory's lap, Hilda would laugh remembering the college-age salesgirls her first husband had paraded around in his restored '57 Chevy. She missed nothing about their marriage, except perhaps the

95

pool in back of their house, into the deep end of which Gregory had jumped that night and stayed for ten minutes, buddy-breathing into a plastic bag.

Certain of winning, Hilda had already turned on the oven by the time Gregory emerged from the water with a turkey who, though trembling badly after its first lesson, was very much alive.

CATALOG

This is the year of you, in all your incarnations. On the cover, you're gliding on a bicycle down a shallow tree-lined hill or lying on a beach with your radio or picking apples or having a snowball fight. You're American, proud and free. Free to spend your money on the bright and beautiful and completely unnecessary things we're about to show you. Free to charge exorbitant amounts on your Visa, Discover, or Mastercard and not think twice about it. In fact, don't think about it even once. We're going to dazzle you with visions of who you could be if you would only try harder.

OUR GUARANTEE
You will be obsessed with every item purchased for at least 24 hours, or we'll provide you with a full refund. Less shipping, of course.

OUR CREED
Even losers and ugly people have the right to buy cool, stylish stuff!

SPRING
Spring is all about becoming the person you imagine when you look in the mirror: laid-back hipster, perky patriot, soccer mom, saucy seductress. But remember, you can't do it without

us. See the fun we're having watching ducklings in the pond or reading a book in bed or hiking in the foothills? We all have our mouths open. Our teeth are preternaturally white. We're happy, so happy, or pleasantly pensive, or surprised by something we see off in the distance. A man, perhaps, pissing against a tree, his face turned toward us, smiling.

Here is your favorite model. You are drawn to her because she is everything you're not—tall and willowy, with naturally curly hair and flawless olive skin. Her arms are not too short for her body, and her breasts don't droop. She does not have a loop of fat around her hips, and when she wears a swimsuit, her thighs are smooth and hairless, and there is a space between them. Her expression is open and friendly; she has a dimple in each cheek. Sometimes you confuse her with yourself, and when you glimpse your real reflection in a glass door or the window of your car, you feel surprised and cheated. You feel so much prettier than that. Everything your favorite model wears you will want. She doesn't have a name, because she is you.

Look! Here you are asleep in a hammock draped with our **Premiercomfort Peace of Mind Lightweight Quilt®**. Your ringlets frame your high, flat cheekbones then cascade past the edge of the hammock, which is suspended over a swimming pool. Can you imagine feeling so safe, so secure, so loved by a quilt that you know it will keep you from making one false move—rolling out of the hammock and into the water below, perhaps, or scolding your daughter in public, or telling your husband you might not love him anymore, like you did just the other day. After you said it, his face collapsed as though gravity had suddenly gotten the better of him, and then you had to take it back and cook him a special dinner and consent to sex even though you didn't feel like it.

Imagine having a quilt that keeps you from saying the wrong thing or from worrying about danger and abandonment or from longing for the many, many things you don't have. Imagine sleeping soundly while wrapped in the unparalleled comfort of our ultimate bedding, which features an absorbent pima cotton cover and synthetic down fill suitable for all seasons. (Except summer, of course. Unless you live in Canada. And who does?)

Catalog number: 12345

Sizes: Twin $100, Twin Extra Long $200, Full $300, Full Extra Long $400, Queen $500, Queen Extra Long $600, King $700, King Extra Long $800

Colors: White, Celery, Patriot, Chartreuse, Teal

Transparent-Toe Sneakers
Here you are again, traipsing down a sunny lane hand-in-hand with a male model who resembles your boyfriend from high school. (Why did you two ever break up, anyway? Why did you marry someone whose chin and ass and hair disappear a little more with each passing year? Don't you deserve better?) Your feet are cradled in our trademark sneakers, which feature cushioned footbeds, rubber three-inch platform soles, and floral scratch-n-sniff decals. (We won't mention that walking in these shoes might be difficult at first and that you might find yourself tripping violently and often on cracks in the sidewalk. We won't mention it because we know there must be a special someone, like the man in the picture, who will hold your hand and act as if he doesn't notice your clumsiness, unlike your best friend, who, when you fell to your knees while leaving the café where you had just had lunch together, hooted and then clapped her hand

over her mouth. She pretended to care that your leggings were ripped at both knees and that blood was trickling out, but you were certain your misfortune and humiliation had made her happy, as it had made you secretly happy when she told you her husband was having an affair with the cashier at the health food store.)

The transparent plastic domes in these unique sneakers reveal your glimmering toenails, painted the purple of Easter eggs to mask your nail fungus. At the windows of the houses lining the street, begonias and pansies and impatiens overflow the window boxes, and on the sidewalk, you and your hunky yet sensitive companion are laughing together at a joke so purely funny and free of malice, you can't even imagine what it might be. You feel superior naturally, without making fun of your work supervisors or your neighbors or even each other. You don't need to gossip or yell at your nine-year-old daughter about cleaning her room, since you are certain she will do it on her own without being told. You no longer feel guilty or hostile or lonely. Wouldn't everyone like to be in your shoes?

Catalog number: 12399

Full and half-sizes 5–12: $125

Colors: Begonia, Pansy, Impatience

Luck o' the Irish

Being born flawed and underprivileged can really take its toll on a girl, but it's nothing a little boost of co-opted luck can't cure. Our four-leaf clover starter kit includes soil packet, mini spade, unbreakable clay pot and a packet of seeds descended from stock gathered over hundreds of years by folksy, dirty Irish shepherds. If cared for properly, these seeds will sprout enough good fortune to get you through the St. Paddy's Day parade (you won't black out this year!), your daughter's third-quarter report card (straight As!), your annual review (a 7% percent raise!), summer vacation (your best friend has gained weight!), your high school reunion (the prom queen remembers you fondly!), and the holiday season.

Catalog number: 12401

$10,000.95

No returns, no refunds

SUMMER

This summer is all about your transformation from caterpillar to butterfly. Our warm-weather clothes and accessories are made especially to mask your potbelly and cheesy thighs. So lie back on your lounger, enjoy your status as newly single, and let us do the really hard work of making you look as if you make more than ten dollars an hour after working eight years for the same market research company, as though you shop somewhere other than Fashion Bug, as though your daughter hasn't taken all the joy out of your divorce by deciding to live with her father instead of you.

Our Exclusive Sheer Marvelsuit®
Wasn't it just yesterday that you and the gang would slide into the country club swimming pool after hours, wearing nothing but your birthday suits? (Never a member of the country club? *Quel dommage.* Think of the pond then, or the river, on those days when the bacteria count allowed for swimming.) Remember the silken thrill of the water on your secret places and how the boys were always trying to get closer? Remember how you would always let your best

friend's boyfriend get just a little too close? Those days don't have to be over. Our **Marvelsuit**® gives the word *skinny-dipping* a whole new meaning.

This radical new swimwear is made of a sheer nylon/Lycra blend lined with a whisper-thin layer of woven steel, so it can mold your sagging breasts and behind into some semblance of the ideal female form, as well as shoring up the extra pounds you gained this spring when all you did was sit on the couch crying over reruns of *Grey's Anatomy* and eating entire bags of Lay's while it rained outside and your husband and his attorney filled out the divorce papers. Even relationships that seem perfect from the outside can be rife with feelings of betrayal and unfulfilled longing, you told your mother long-distance. Sometimes a girl must finally face the fact that her husband is the source and symbol of everything that's wrong with her life.

But consider what you have to look forward to: splashing in sapphire shallows with a man who looks suspiciously like your best friend's husband and who obviously can't resist you in your Marvelsuit®. Once you're in it, you'll want to stay all day. In the evening when you pry yourself out of this revolutionary swimwear, don't mind the depressions—the grooves and pock marks will most likely disappear by morning. The cramps will dissipate in less than an hour, and you'll feel like eating again by suppertime. Just think of the pennies and pounds you've saved by skipping lunch!

Hand wash; do not microwave.

Made in the USA by USWA.
Catalog number: 12480

Sizes XS–XXL: $300

Colors: Sheer Black & Blue, Sheer Red, Sheer Nude

Pair with our **Modest Mesh Cover-Up** (p. 34)

ONE-TIME SAVINGS
This between-seasons special mailing is all about you helping us make a profit on the mistakes we've made this year.
Here, you'll save 1–10% on selected merchandise, and you'll
feel lucky to snatch it up without considering that these are
the items no one else wanted because they're hideous and/
or unwearable.

Garbage-Bag Maillot
This slippery, shiny one-piece swimsuit is inspired by the
exotic yet practical economies of many Third World coun-
tries and will have you feeling like a fish in water. Here
you are wearing the landfill green maillot, lying back on
one elbow with your knees twisted sideways. Your smile is
a little less friendly than usual, probably because today is
your thirty-fifth birthday, and every night lately before you
go to sleep alone in the big bed you used to share with your
husband, you wonder why no one has asked you for a date.
It's been nearly four months since he moved out, and you
have broadcast the news widely—to friends, coworkers, the
cashiers at the grocery store—that you are single again, even
though it's true that you can't stand men in general—you
couldn't even put up with a kind, caring man like your soon-
to-be ex-husband, who was always bringing you coffee in
bed in the morning, always asking, "What's wrong, honey?"
and "Won't you talk to me about what's bothering you?"

Did you make a mistake filing for divorce? You feel like the
world—and even God—has cheated you in so many ways by
making it impossible for you to feel satisfied with anything.
You can't decide what would make you feel better: getting
your facial hair waxed or calling your best friend's husband
at work to see if he wants to meet you somewhere for lunch.

Maybe you are just angry at being included in the sale catalog. The photographer probably arranged you in this uncomfortable pose and while he was doing so noticed that the slippery swimsuit was creeping up your behind and that your thighs aren't quite as firm as they were when you were thirty-four. Bastard! Your rage makes your favorite model's hair shinier, makes her skin glow as if lit from inside by a golden lantern.

Catalog number: 12723

Sizes XXXXS–S

Indicate Cinch-Sack, Ziploc or Twist-Tie neckline

Regular Price: $150.00

Sale Price: $139.50

Colors: Landfill Green (shown), White

Neon Gingham 'n' Stripes Picnic Set
Perk up your picnics with this sassy collection. Rainbow-gingham-lined basket includes matching picnic blanket and four brilliant lime plates, cups, forks, knives and spoons, as well as four gingham napkins in grape, geranium, orange sherbet and electric banana. If you had this picnic set, you could invite your daughter and almost-ex-husband on a picnic. Your husband would take one bite of your famous potato salad and exclaim, "I refuse to divorce a woman who can make potato salad like this," though he's eaten it many times before. He would pull the divorce papers from the back pocket of his perennial Lee jeans and rip them into tiny pieces that would flutter and tumble into the grass beyond the blinding picnic blanket.

We're pretending this unattractive item is a steal at 10% off the regular price.

Catalog number: 12750

Regular Price: $125.00

Sale Price: $112.50

Toddler Thong (pictured above), see **page 21**.

FALL
You'll never be more *you* than you are this fall, wearing our **Ace-Bandage Turtleneck** and watching your best friend's husband play soccer in the park while you sit in the bleachers next to your best friend's cousin, whom you began dating out of a desperate attempt not to spend the coldest months of the year alone. He's a loud, burly man who is enthusiastic enough in bed for both of you.

Catalog number: 12592

Sizes XS–M: $123

Colors: Pumpkin, Squash, Sunflower Seed

Must-Have Lightweight Sweater
Cool, crisp days call for warm, elegant and sometimes itchy fabrics. Here you are sitting on a hay bale wearing our Must-Have Cardigan, an exclusive blend of organic lambswool and assorted dried field grasses. Do we need to remind you that looking good is worth a little physical discomfort?
Catalog number: 12890

Indicate Cardigan, Turtleneck, or Halter

Sizes S–XXXXXL: $250

Colors: (shown opposite) Knoll, Butte, Field, Pond, Puddle

Corduroy Trousers
There's a kind of peace you can only know in a pair of plush corduroy trousers. Our cords come in three styles, one of

which is guaranteed to fill that gaping vacuum you call your spiritual life. Be warned, however—choose the wrong style for your body type, and these trousers will ride up after washing, emphasize your thick waist or make your ass look like a satchel full of rocks.

Here is your favorite model looking slim and leggy in the Flat Front style, which you won't admit wouldn't suit your short legs and rounded paunch. You notice that in this photograph the makeup artist has highlighted your cheekbones, forehead and chin with warm autumn colors, perhaps to mask your pallor. Ever since you turned thirty-five and officially became a divorcée, you have fallen back into old habits, like bingeing on and purging entire sticks of salami, sucking on the ends of your hair, and picking at your toenail fungus with a sewing needle.

Catalog number: 12907

Indicate Mom Butt, Flat Front, or Camel Toe

Sizes XS–M: $89.00

Sizes L–XL: $99.00

Colors: Golden Lab (pictured above), Pine Forest, Twinkletoes, Autumn Sumac, Turkey Trot, Melancholia

Measure to make sure!
Finding the right size is easy with our patented Mez-U-Rite® system.

Women's Size Guide

	Size	Bust	Waist	Hips
XS	0–4	0–33"	0–25"	0–35"
S	6–7	34 ½ –35 ½"	26 ¾–27 ¾"	36 ⅝–37 ⅝"
M	11–13	38–38 ½"	30–31"	39–39 ¾"
L	14–19	39–44"	33–36 ⅞"	41 ½–46 ¾"
XL	21	44 ½"	37"	47"
XXL	22–24	46 ½–48 ½"	39–41"	49–51"
XXXL	26–28	50–70"	45–80"	55"–infinity

WINTER

Winter is all about reflecting on a subject dear to your heart—you! Your life unfolds, a patchwork of ice and snow, holiday hopes and New Year fantasies, maxed-out credit cards, manipulation and insecurity, agoraphobia and depression. We're here to capitalize on your Seasonal Affective Disorder in a way that makes us seem generous. After all, feeling bad about yourself doesn't mean you have to dress poorly! Because we care, our products are made especially for you. So what if you pay ten to fifteen times what it actually costs the sweatshops to make them? How can something cost too much when your well-being is at stake? Isn't your happiness more important than money?

Capri Snow Pants
Be ahead of the curve, with a smile on your face and snow in your socks. Nylon shell, Tinfoil® liner. Machine wash.

Catalog number: 12989

Sizes S–XXL: $150

Colors: (shown above) Blue Sky, Gray River, Yellow Snow

The Way Life Should Be®
Finally, a way to reminisce without contemplating suicide! Button up our **Bedtime for Bonzo Flannel Pajamas (p. 51)**, curl up on our **Special Edition Fur-n-Leather Sofa (p. 60)**, then slip on our **Lightning-Action Headset®** and let your memory absorb the poignant, humorous and sexually arousing incidents that would have filled your life, were there any justice in the world. Settings include "Funny Times," "Blessings in Disguise," "101 Unbelievable Orgasms," "Functional Family of Origin," and "Great Moments in Sports."

Catalog number: 12999

$3,500.00

Slouching Toward the Gym Bag

You haven't exercised since God knows when. Face it—you're a fat, lazy pig. No wonder your husband left you (which is what you've been telling people lately and what you've almost come to believe) and your best friend's cousin decided you should just be friends. Having this elegant carryall in the back of your closet means there's hope that one day you will have the intelligence and force of will to sign up for those aerobics classes—or at least get on the elliptical trainer, for God's sake. Or maybe you can just take this bag out of your closet from time to time and caress its sturdy leatherette strap and unbreakable zipper, plunge your hands into the deodorized satin interior and finger the pockets made especially for your sneakers and lipstick. So what if it costs more than a yearly membership at the Y?

Look! Here you are crossing a snow-lined street on your way to the gym. You wear a dreamily distracted smile, the result of the Valium you persuaded your doctor to prescribe. Your curly hair pokes out adorably from beneath your **Floppy Fleece Sou'wester (p. 30)** in burnt orange, a color that looks great on your favorite model but would really only make you look jaundiced. Your **Slightly Flared Jeans (p. 10)** look perfect with your **Wedgie Moonboots (p. 41)**, but you are not truly happy. Things haven't turned out quite the way you planned. You miss your daughter terribly, even the mess she used to make with peanut butter and jelly on the kitchen counter and the way she would cry if you so much as looked at her cross-eyed.

Sometimes when it's not your weekend, you throw on a pair of sweatpants after work and go pick up some takeout then find yourself driving past the apartment building where your daughter and ex-husband now live. Of course, it won't be long before the old house where you all used to live together, where you now live alone, sells for an appreciable profit and you move into a condo, where your young, handsome next-door neighbor will show you for the first time how fulfilling sex can be. He'll know just how to handle you, how to pull you from this place inside yourself where you are mired, a perspective from which everything in the world appears to be stacked against you. He will love your daughter, and she will have much more fun with him than she ever had with her father. Soon she'll want to move back in with you, and, of course, you'll allow it.

Tonight you'll order a little something for yourself from the catalog, and tomorrow you'll call a Realtor and begin your search for a condo in a building with an exercise room. You couldn't possibly let your new boyfriend see you naked like this.

Catalog number: 13001

Colors: Teal (exterior)/Mauve (interior), Black/White, Hugs/ Kisses, Harmony/Contentment

$400.00

ROMANCE

You fit the box fan into your bedroom window, facing out toward the yard so you can blow the smoke from your cigarette through it, so your parents can pretend not to notice. You're reading a romance novel in bed, a ritual that means more to you than anything that goes on at school or in the church services your parents drag you to on Sundays. Your heart aches for the heroine—this one is a wallflower, but some of them are spitfires, and all of them are just like you. Someday you, too, will fall in love with a brutally handsome Dominic or Edgar or Logan, a rugged, secretly kindhearted man with a will strong enough to tame your own.

"Charming," he says of the brash way you talk to your friends on the phone. "Oh, darling, stop," he says when you throw a shoe at your little sister and tell her to get the hell out of your room.

You are saving yourself for him.

After the inevitable happy ending, after chores—scrubbing molding bathtub caulk and vacuuming nappy carpeting—you call Jane, who arrives in her Nissan with rusting edges. The two of you are spending the night at Amanda's house in the coulee while her parents are away—as they often are, leaving Amanda and her brother on their own. Nothing your parents need to know.

All afternoon, you ride Amanda's horses bareback through the wooded hills. You are in love with the warm afternoon, with the feeling of holding the bay mare between your thighs, with the roll and ripple of her cantering under a tree while you scream with joy and lie against her neck as the low branches snag your silky hair.

The sun goes down, and you dress for the party in Amanda's bedroom, which still has ruffled curtains and a yellow canopy over the bed. You wear Amanda's jean shorts and a pink-striped tank top. Amanda wears Jane's sundress and your Roman sandals, and Jane wears Amanda's gauzy blouse and your miniskirt. None of you wears a bra. You flip your hair in the mirror. You share a cigarette and then reapply bubblegum lip gloss as cars pull into the driveway and the boys burst through the back door with the barrel.

Later, staggering into the dark leather study, passing out on the sofa. Then something pulling you up out of oblivion, and at the surface, Amanda's brother, Craig, is breathing on your face; his hands are taking off your clothes, moving your doll's limbs. Light coming in from the hallway like the beam of a flashlight: *I see you.*

The next day, Craig is somehow your boyfriend, though you've never liked him that way, and the reflection of yourself you saw in the mirror yesterday has shattered without anyone noticing but you. The pieces of yourself are there on the floor, but when you try to make sense of them, one refracting sunbeam after another hits you directly in the eye.

OBSCURE MAGIC

I

HOW VERY LILTS TOOK HER DAUGHTER

AND LEFT THE VORACIOUS WORLD

Once, in a faraway land called the Thumb of Michigan, there was a walled estate that rose up like a castle from the plain. The famous author Very Lilts lived there, with her daughter and a large security staff. Vee had suffered paranoid fits ever since her husband—the magician Ever Lilts—their infant daughter, and their nephew had vanished, leaving her penniless and pregnant with their second child. Someone had taken her family, but a police investigation turned up nothing. They seemed to have vanished into thin air.

Vee wrote a memoir about her experience that was a selection for Oprah's Book Club and an international bestseller. She met a psychic who could not tell her where they had gone but did predict, unbidden, that her second daughter would grow up beautiful and wise, and that she, too, would disappear, at eighteen.

The prediction sent Vee into a rage. For her, the world had become a voracious creature, one that would swallow everything she loved. With the proceeds from the memoir and her subsequent series of dark suspense novels filled with traitors and backstabbers, she bought a cornfield outside Marlette, built the huge fortified stone house there, and shut her daughter and herself up inside it. She had her husband's magical compass set in the wall near the main entrance to prevent anyone from finding the estate unless invited.

II

HOW THE GIRL ALMOST DISCOVERED A MYSTERIOUS WOODS, AND WHAT THE GARDENER SAID ABOUT IT

The child grew to be almost as beautiful and wise as predicted, but her natural curiosity made her nose a little long, and her quiet demeanor meant she often went unnoticed by the musicians and performers Vee invited to stay at the estate for weeks at a time. They didn't mind the security measures or the fact that, between visits, they couldn't quite remember where the estate was located.

Almost learned to read at a young age and, full of stories, began to wonder what type of protagonist she might turn out to be. She wasn't sweet and beloved by everyone like Little Red Cap or Snow White and Rose Red, but neither was she cruel like the princess was to the frog king or lazy like the daughter who lied about being able to spin. Maybe she was like the protagonists who got by on their wits, but she didn't like this option, for these were the protagonists in the scariest stories. Would a murderous suitor disguised as a beggar persuade her to open the door and carry her away in his enchanted basket? She had inherited her mother's fear of the outside world, as surely as she had inherited her brown eyes and wavy brown hair, and she swore to never leave her mother's house, to never even open the door.

But she had heard of the psychic's warning, and just in case that future did come, she listened carefully to what her teachers said about the outside world and studied everything she could get her hands on: books from the library, catalogs that came in the mail, the few television shows and movies she was allowed to watch, and the websites she was allowed to visit. She wanted to know as much as she could about the world, a place she learned was rife with Meijer stores and McDonald's, mass shootings and 7-Eleven Big Gulps, countless communication breakdowns and cases of unrequited love. She spent hours watching from her bedroom window the cars and trucks and school buses that passed on the road. She asked for a spotting scope, ostensibly to observe wildlife, and she did use it to watch birds and deer and weasels, but she also watched the faces of the children inside the buses on their way to school, the lines on their palms pressed against the windows.

The Thumb landscape stretched beyond the highway, flat and covered in farm fields and dotted with occasional stands of trees, including one patch of forest that made Almost think of a certain young security guard's goatee, the bristly black hair that sprang from his otherwise smooth face. The security guard, Tab, lived at the edge of that patch of woods in an Airstream trailer that glinted in the sun.

Almost had discovered Tab's address by accident, when one day she found that she could follow his truck with the scope after he left the driveway and turned right onto the highway and then turned left down a dirt road. Throughout the winter, Almost set her alarm early so that she could watch Tab emerge from the Airstream each morning. The first thing he did was make his way into the woods, despite the signs nailed to the trees on the perimeter that read,

"Trespassers Will Be Violated. This Means You." She wondered who owned the land—perhaps a witch or a murderous robber—and what would happen if Tab were caught there.

Season after season, as she watched him disappear among the trees, an overwhelming curiosity welled up in her about this strange place where no tree or flower or grass ever bloomed. Every time he went in, her own desire to go there grew a little stronger, in spite of her fears.

She questioned the gardener, Therefore, about the woods one day in early fall.

"It's been winter there for many years, since before you were born," Therefore said. "The blood has frozen in the veins of the trees."

"But haven't you been there?" Almost asked.

Something like the sun was inside the gardener. Heat seeped through their clothing, carrying the smell of grass and soil. Almost had seen plants grow just because Therefore looked at them, had stood by and watched the leaves of the prayer plant lift and rest against each other in response to their breath.

"I went there when you were a baby," Therefore said and shrugged. "I can't really say anything more about it."

Vee called to Almost shrilly from the shady side of the atrium. The vertical creases between her eyebrows were visible even from a distance.

"What was Therefore saying to you?" she asked tersely as Almost sat down at the table for lunch.

Almost shrugged. "They want me to pick the asparagus."

"I've got a funny feeling about them," Vee said. She was always saying things like that about Therefore, even though they had known each other since Therefore worked at the garden center in Marlette, before Almost was born. Vee's eyes darted around the table now as though the vegetables from Therefore's garden might be poisoned, or wired.

Vee's paranoia was contagious, and Almost had the jitters as her eighteenth birthday approached. She considered that leaving the estate would allow her to visit the woods that never bloomed. The urge to go there tugged against the opposite urge to stay with her mother forever, as though staying might ease her mother's tortured mind.

III

HOW, YEARS AGO, LOVE OF MUSIC BROUGHT ALMOST'S PARENTS TOGETHER

There was nothing Vee loved more than music, and when she and Almost listened together, Vee could relax and forget for a short time the traumas of the past and the terror awaiting her in the future. If she drank a glass of wine during a good concert, afterward she might bring out her photo albums and tell Almost stories of the old days.

She and Almost's father had met in a folk club where he was playing guitar at the open mic. "Magic was your father's vocation, but he did also love playing his guitar."

When they were first married and he was perfecting his act as the Amazing Mr. Lilts, they lived in a roach-infested apartment in Detroit. But it wasn't long before Ever, who was a natural magician (everyone agreed he had the best cups and balls routine anyone had ever seen) began to fraternize with the more famous magicians. (According to Vee, the other illusionists only pretended to support her husband. She was convinced that some of them had conspired to disappear him.)

Ever was able to book higher-paying gigs. They moved into a better apartment. Then they got the bad news: Ever's brother and sister-in-law had died in a fire, leaving their son an orphan. Ever and Vee became Soon's legal wards.

Almost studied the photos of her cousin wearing a magician's top hat and flourishing a white-tipped wand. Soon loved magic, and Almost's father took him under his wing. He called him his little apprentice. But Vee and Ever saw that Soon wasn't thriving in the city, and they took him back to Marlette, where he had lived when his parents were alive. Vee and Ever bought a white bungalow on Morris Street.

How happy they had all been to learn that a little baby was on the way!

"Your father would sing to your sister before she was born," Vee told Almost, "and she would move when she heard his voice."

Vee had digital recordings of Almost's father singing, his melody sometimes interwoven with Vee's own lush soprano harmony. Though Vee never sang again after her husband's disappearance, she welcomed musicians into her home, and different bands of them could be found roaming the estate. Currently, Vee was partial to bagpipes, and her music planner was at his wits' end trying to find players who would stay year-round.

Almost loved music too, and she felt inspired to sing along to many familiar songs, but she suspected her mother would disapprove. She only dared sing in secret, in her bedroom, with Spotify turned up to hide the sound.

IV

HOW TAB THE SECURITY GUARD AND ALMOST
BECAME SECRETLY ACQUAINTED

The day before Almost's eighteenth birthday, Tab was on the rotation of guards reporting her whereabouts every thirty minutes, as Vee had ordered.

He appeared in the morning at the base of the climbing wall where Almost was halfway to the top.

"Eyes on the prize," he said into the two-way radio clipped to his shoulder. "Currently flagging her left foot."

Almost lost her balance at the sound of Tab's voice and hung above him in her harness as his dark brown eyes sprinkled their stardust over her.

After he let go of the button on his radio, Tab asked, "Everything all right here?"

"Yes, thank you," Almost said, lowering herself to the ground. Her eyes appreciated his sturdy form, his broad shoulders and muscular arms and legs.

The two of them had been conducting a secret conversation for nearly a year, a few sentences at a time.

He stroked his goatee now to hide his mouth from the surveillance cameras. "I have a surprise for your birthday," he said, and Almost's stomach flipped. Then he was gone, continuing his patrol route.

Tab found her an hour later in the library trying, but failing, to focus on her anatomy and physiology homework, labeling the parts of the circulatory system. After reporting her whereabouts and activities, Tab bent as if to tie his boot and said, "Meet me here in the library tomorrow morning at nine."

She feigned a yawn into her hand. "I can't possibly."

The next hour, Tab found her in the kitchen pantry, where she was looking for a snack. She stood with the pantry door pulled almost closed, where no camera could see her, and directed a luxurious stream of words at him. "We'll be caught immediately," she said, "and that's not how I want to spend my birthday, with Vee in a rage over how I've betrayed her."

Tab pretended to sweep the room for listening devices. He ran his hand along the baseboards. "Oh, I have a plan," he said into his armpit. They had developed a distilled form of communication, and when Tab patted the pocket of his uniform pants, Almost knew that he had devised a way to administer a sleeping potion to the day shift, the guests, and even to Vee.

V

HOW ALMOST CAME TO VIOLATE

HER MOTHER'S INVIOLABLE RULE, IN SPITE OF HERSELF

Almost decided she would meet Tab the next morning at nine and tell him that she had no intention of leaving the estate. It would only exacerbate Vee's mental illness, which was the main thing that kept her and Almost from being close like so many mothers and daughters in the movies on the Hallmark Channel.

When Almost came out of her room in the morning, as usual, she found the guard in the hallway curled up on the padded bench across from her door. She ran to the south atrium, where her mother liked to have breakfast and read the paper on the patio in the flower garden. Her mother was there, asleep with her elbow on the table, her face propped in her hand. The members of the string quartet that had been playing nearby were also asleep in their chairs, the cellist snoring softly as she held her instrument close.

Almost's heart was racing by the time she reached the library, where Tab waited, leaning against a table. The air between them filled with sparks, like the fireflies Almost had seen from her window. Then Tab's arms were around her, and he was kissing her, and Almost was kissing him back, and she was so caught up in the sensations his lips invoked that she hardly noticed when he reached up to touch the charm on the necklace she had never noticed he wore tucked inside his uniform shirt. In the silver wink of an eye, they were in the outside world, in back of the estate, beyond the wall.

Almost's poor mother had been right to worry about her disappearing, and Almost felt sad and sorry but also glad and free as the morning breeze touched her face and lifted her hair. The sky was impossibly high, its massive white midsummer clouds like mountains, and she was grateful that Tab held her hand so that she didn't float away.

VI

HOW ALMOST SPENT HER FIRST DAY
IN THE OUTSIDE WORLD

Almost disembarked unsteadily from Tab's pickup in the Thumb town of Port Austin, reeling from the speed with which they had traveled north on M-53. It was Saturday, and the air smelled of coffee and popcorn. The center of the town was filled with people attending the farmers' market, more people than Almost had ever seen in one place, strolling past the booths of fresh vegetables and baked goods, jam and honey, pickles, cheese, and meat. She looked carefully at everyone and everything, at first because of lingering para-noia but then because she wanted to remember every detail for the rest of her life, to take them out and page through them the way she paged through her mother's photo albums.

She and Tab drank coffee and ate croissants as they walked along the streets of Port Austin. Then they caught a tour boat to Turnip Rock, which emerged from the clear green water of Lake Huron like an enchanted root vegetable, the trees sprouting from its top like turnip greens. Everyone on the boat was talking at once, turning their faces to the wind, and Almost wanted to bottle their conversations to preserve the sound of their laughter, to drink it later. She stood at the rail, shoulder to shoulder with Tab, squinting as though it would allow her to see the other side of the lake.

After lunch at a beachside restaurant, they walked along the rocky shoreline past Pointe Aux Barques. Away from the crowds, Almost felt shy as she looked out at the vast expanse of water, felt the soothing rhythm of the waves, felt how impossible it would be to ever thank Tab for such a gift.

"We should get back," Tab said, throwing his arm across her shoulders. "The potion will be wearing off soon."

Almost's mood deflated at the thought of going back inside her mother's estate. This day had somehow felt like the first real day of her life, and her life at Vee's estate now seemed more like a dream.

Tab squeezed her shoulder. Then he held something out to her, dropped into her hand a rock that fit perfectly in the bowl of her palm. A smooth white rock shaped roughly like a heart and studded with smaller deep-orange and dark gray rocks.

"It's beautiful," she said, her fingers appreciating its smooth surface.

"Puddingstone," Tab said. "It's metamorphic—made by fire."

There were the sparks again, between them. Almost slipped the rock into her pocket. Her first birthday present.

VII

HOW ALMOST WAS NEARLY LOST ON HER WAY HOME

Tab stopped for gas on the way out of Port Austin, and Almost went into the tiny store to use the bathroom. On her way, she saw an elderly man push open the door of his ancient gold Cadillac in the parking lot. Hadn't she seen the same car in a parking lot near the farmers' market? The man planted a four-footed cane on the ground, heaved himself up out of the driver's seat, and began his slow, hunched journey toward the store. He was wearing, oddly, a fur coat that looked as if it had seen better days. His hair was a strange white thatch. When Almost came back out of the store, the old man had just reached the curb, where he didn't lift the cane high enough and so caught one of the rubber tips, which caused him to stumble and fall to his knees on the sidewalk.

He seemed to fall in slow motion, and Almost was able to catch him by the furry forearms before he fell forward onto his face. A flash in her mind of Goldilocks encountering the bears.

"Are you all right, sir?" she asked. "Do you think you can stand?"

"Yes, yes, my dear. Thank you," he said in a weak raspy voice that smelled surprisingly of mothballs, as though his voice had been packed away in a trunk—or was that the coat? His hair and face looked so odd, and Almost tried not to stare. Was he in disguise? Why else would he be wearing this bad wig? Why else would his face be caked with such a thick layer of stage makeup? She helped him to his feet and brushed the dust from the knees of his fraying wool trousers.

"I'm Mr. Still," he said, and she looked into his dark eyes, which had an uncanny depth, a sort of gravitational pull. She felt lost for a moment.

"I wonder if I could trouble you for one more thing," he said. "You see, I just realized that I've left my billfold in the car. Would you fetch it for me? It's such a long way for an old fellow." He smiled at her, his dry lips drawing back to reveal teeth stained yellow and brown.

"Of course!" Almost said. She felt a surge of eagerness to help this man. As soon as she was certain he could stand without assistance, she took the keys he offered.

"I keep it under the passenger seat," he said. "You can't be too careful."

Almost used the car key to open the passenger door of the gold Cadillac and then crouched to feel under the seat for the billfold, but she couldn't find it. It was a mystery to her how Mr. Still would even be able to put it under there in the first place. She got into the passenger seat and was reaching as far as she could underneath it when, in a rush of stale air, someone was suddenly there in the driver's seat. Almost looked up to see Mr. Still sitting next to her, the car keys dangling from his hand. How in the world had he made it back to the car so quickly? As she looked into his eyes once more, his dark irises seemed to spin.

Then someone grabbed her right arm, and she jumped violently. It was Tab. He pulled her out of the car while reaching inside the neck of his T-shirt for the silver charm he had used that morning, and in the wink of an eye, she and he were in the cab of his pickup truck, and he was speeding away from the Port Austin Shell station, south on M-53. Almost sat stunned for several miles. What had just happened? Who had fastened her seatbelt? And why did she keep forgetting to ask Tab about the silver charm that hung on the chain around his neck?

"Who is Mr. Still?" Almost asked when she finally found her voice again.

Tab looked over at her. "Let's just say your mother's fears about the outside world are not necessarily unwarranted," he said.

"Why didn't you tell me?"

He shrugged. "I wanted you to enjoy your birthday—and I guess I got a little complacent." He offered her a huge plastic ICEE cup filled to the top of the clear dome with blue raspberry ice, and she accepted it with both hands. She didn't realize until much later that he had never answered her question about Mr. Still.

VIII

HOW ALMOST WAS BANISHED FROM HER MOTHER'S ESTATE

When Almost and Tab winked back into the library at Vee's estate, appearing on the same spot from which they had left, the room was filled with orange-gold afternoon light. Almost was flooded with equal parts relief and regret to be home again.

"I don't know how I'll ever thank you," she said to Tab and threw her arms around his neck and kissed him.

Just then the door to the library banged open, and Vee stumbled across the threshold, squinting in the sunlight. "How sweet," she said as Almost stepped out of Tab's embrace. Vee's eyes were deranged with what someone else might mistake for murderous rage but Almost knew was fear for Almost's life.

Vee pointed at Tab with a long finger whose nail she had bitten to the quick. "You're fired," she said. "You'll be lucky if I don't sue you for kidnapping and breach of contract."

"Oh, Mother." Almost sighed. "I'm sorry to have scared you. But I'm all right."

"You—" Her mother's voice broke. "You want to live Outside, live Outside. You have one hour to get out of my house."

I'm the kind of protagonist, Almost thought with dry-eyed resignation, *who enters the world with her mother's footprint on her backside.*

In the hallway, surrounded by guards, Tab asked Almost to come and stay with him until she decided what her next steps would be. Almost thought of the wide world, the people and shops and restaurants, the farms and gardens, the boats and endless lakes. She nodded, and Tab said that he would pick her up out front this time.

IX

HOW, BEFORE THE DAY ENDED, ALMOST RECEIVED
TWO MORE BIRTHDAY GIFTS, FOR A TOTAL OF THREE

Almost persuaded the guards to take her to Therefore's apartment before she gathered her things. When she explained to the gardener what had happened, they embraced her, and then they reached into the pocket of their robe and pulled out a small cloth bag tied with a bright pink ribbon, as though they had been expecting Almost. When they put the bag into Almost's hand, she could feel that it was filled with seeds.

"From the flowers here," they said.

Her second birthday gift.

In her room, Almost put the seeds, a change of clothes, her iPod, and her laptop into her backpack. The guards took her by her mother's suite to see if Vee wanted to say goodbye, but Almost found the rooms there empty. She picked up an embroidery ring that lay on the table beside Vee's bed. The needle contained black thread, but there were no stitches in the linen yet, only three spots of blood on the white cloth. Her mother must have pricked herself. Almost released the cloth from the hoop, wrapped the threaded needle in it, and put the bundle into her pack. She counted it as her third birthday gift.

She and Tab drove out through the front gate, and Almost looked back once more at her mother's house, where the lights were coming up as the sun sank below the horizon. Soon the estate would be as brightly lit as a birthday cake. Her mother had said, "You have one hour to get out of my house." It had never been Almost's house, never her life.

She and Tab got dinner at Taco Bell and then went home to the Airstream. When Tab turned onto the dirt road that led to his campsite, a shiver started at the nape of Almost's neck and ran like a spider up into her hair. Could it be that she would finally go into the sleeping forest?

X

HOW ALMOST FINALLY ENTERED THE WOOD
THAT NEVER BLOOMED, AND WHAT SHE FOUND THERE

When Almost opened her eyes the next morning, light was leaking in through the windows of the trailer, and Tab was rising from the bunk across from hers and pulling on jeans and a T-shirt. She lay still, pretending sleep, and as soon as he left, she dressed quickly and shrugged into her backpack, wondering why Tab hadn't invited her along. Was he visiting someone in the woods, someone he didn't want her to know about? Jealousy stabbed her heart, a tiny briar.

It was easy to catch up with him by following the sounds of his boots through the brush, and he showed no signs of noticing her. It was freezing in the forest. When Therefore had told her it was always winter there, Almost had not taken it literally. But her breath appeared before her in foggy clouds, and the ground was icy hard. She moved faster through the trees, trying to keep warm. She kept her eyes on Tab, around whom the air suddenly began to glow and tremble. Then he was gone, and in his place a sturdy black cat trotted along, a silver chain gleaming around its neck. The cat flashed a dark-eyed glance at Almost over his shoulder and began to run, diving nimbly through the bare honeysuckle and thorn bushes. In a few seconds, Almost had lost him.

She hesitated. The patch of woods had seemed so small from her bedroom window, and even when she'd walked in, she could have sworn she could see through the trees to the other side. Now the forest seemed to go on forever, and the trees seemed taller, their trunks thicker. When Almost looked back the way she'd come, she could still see the edge of the woods. Perhaps she should turn back now, while she could still find her way. She did not have anything in her pockets to use to mark her path, no stones like Hansel or peas and lentils like the girl betrothed to the robber bridegroom. But she hated to think that she was the kind of protagonist who turned back out of fear.

Just then, a strange wailing began to echo through the trees. It sounded like a baby crying, and it seemed to be coming from everywhere—the tree trunks and the branches and the bushes, even the ground. Almost tried to locate the origin of the noise. She closed her eyes and wandered toward it until she found herself in a wide clearing on the far side of which stood a dwarfed tree, thick-trunked but barely six feet tall. As she got closer, Almost was sure the cries were coming from inside it. But when she started toward the tree, a boy with a dirty face, wearing a ragged corduroy coat stepped out from behind it.

"Be on your way," he said in a shrill voice. He couldn't have been more than nine years old. "These woods are mine."

"What's in the tree?" Almost asked him. How was it that his face looked familiar?

"A baby, stupid. Can't you hear her crying?"

He fidgeted with something, passing it from one hand to the other, lifting his hand high and dropping the item into his other hand and then opening the hand to show that it was empty. Almost took a few slow steps toward the boy, and he crouched, as though ready to spring at her.

The wailing was driving Almost mad. How could the boy just stand there while the baby cried? "Can't I see the baby?" she asked.

"No," he said.

He resumed his fidgeting. His lips and fingernails were tinged blue, and Almost wondered how long he and the baby had been in the woods. As she inched closer, she noticed that his coat had no buttons—that it was a button he was passing from hand to hand.

"You know," she said, "I can sew that button back onto your coat."

Her words made the boy strangely, immediately ecstatic; he looked as though he would cry with joy as he pulled from his pocket five more buttons, all of which Almost promptly reattached with her mother's embroidery needle and the black thread.

"There," she said, handing the coat back to the trembling boy. "Now do you believe I'm a friend?"

The boy buttoned his coat and turned the broad collar up over his ears. Then he led Almost to the tree. There was a hollow space in the top of the trunk where the branches parted, and the baby lay there nestled in a heap of blankets. Her mouth was open in a small sucking *O*, her tiny fists jerking as she wailed.

Almost was reaching to pick her up when the black cat— Tab—leaped up onto the tree with a blinding ball of light dangling from his jaws. The baby stopped crying abruptly, and the cat dropped the orb delicately into her mouth.

"That's what she eats," the boy said. "He gets them from the Seer."

Tab jumped from the tree onto Almost's shoulder and rubbed his cheek against her ear, purring loudly. She and the boy laughed. But just as suddenly, Tab leaped down and stood growling as he watched the far edge of the clearing. The hair along his spine was raised like the fin of a fish, and his tail had gone bushy as a hairbrush.

A man emerged noisily from a briar patch. He wore a fur coat matted with dead leaves and burrs, and he was panting as if he'd run a long way. Mr. Still had changed since Almost had seen him at the gas station. He was no longer masquerading as an old man but now looked like a haggard version of her own father. Almost looked sidelong at the boy. Was it possible that he was her cousin Soon? Was it possible that this baby was her sister, who had cried so much after she was born that her parents named her Never Satisfied?

Mr. Still lifted a Starbucks cup to his mouth, took a long swallow from it, and then threw it into the bushes. He spat on the ground, and where his spit landed, shiny agates appeared, reminding Almost of the puddingstone in her pocket.

"I see you've met your sister," Mr. Still said to Almost.

"Soon," Almost said to her cousin, "what is going on?"

"He was cursed," Soon said and pulled Almost by the arm until the two of them stood between Mr. Still and the tree in which the baby lay. "The baby is draining his magic away."

"What does he want?" Almost asked.

"He wants to kill her," Soon said.

Mr. Still began to hum, and, as if on cue, the baby began to wail again. The air vibrated with the harmony of their greed and loneliness and hunger. Almost clapped her hands over her ears, but she could hear Mr. Still's voice when he began to sing in a voice as deep and soothing as the waves on the shore of Lake Huron: *Make me a pallet on your floor. Make me a pallet on your floor. Make it soft, make it low, so my good gal will never know. Make me a pallet on your floor.*

It was one of the folk songs her father had recorded and Vee had played for Almost so many times.

He sang louder, and Almost resisted the urge to fall to her knees: *Come on, you good time friends of mine . . . When I had a dollar, you treated me so fine . . . Where'd you go when I only had a dime?*

Almost watched his mouth move, saw the discolored teeth behind his lips. How could her father's voice be coming from this man, the villain of her story? Mr. Still, as he sang, began to cry, and the tears that fell from his eyes turned to diamonds and emeralds on his cheeks and then clicked onto the frozen ground. He scooped up what he could of them and put them into the pockets of his coat.

He was hunched over that way when he suddenly rushed at Almost and Soon, his arms outstretched and the wings of his fur coat filling with air. Without realizing it, Almost had found the puddingstone and brought it out of her pocket. Now she drew her arm back and threw the stone as hard as she could at Mr. Still. When it hit him, squarely in the heart with a sound like a baseball hitting a glove, he flew backward several yards and landed hard on his back. He lay there without moving.

XI

HOW OBSCURE MAGIC IS SOMETIMES THE RIGHT KIND

Almost knelt next to Mr. Still's inanimate body. He wasn't breathing, and she felt no pulse at his neck. How would she tell her mother that she had killed her own father, the man for whom Vee had been pining all these years? Soon comforted her, saying that maybe the Seer could help. They made a litter using Mr. Still's fur coat tied with ivy vines to a frame of branches, and Almost dragged him behind her while Soon carried the baby. Tab the cat trotted ahead, leading them deeper into the forest, to the Seer's cottage. They left Mr. Still's litter in the yard and stepped inside.

The Seer was an ancient woman with a shrunken face and white permed hair like the Golden Girls. She was sitting on a sofa in her living room eating Kentucky Fried Chicken from a box and watching the *Today* show on a flat-screen TV. A large angular black dog lay in the corner. His tail thumped against the floor when Tab jumped into the Seer's lap and began to lick her greasy fingers. The old woman wiped the shine from her face with a napkin.

"Thank you for coming," she said to Almost. "I sent my grandson Tab to find you. Alas, I'm getting too old for all this excitement. Figure out this spell, undo that curse." She sighed, but she was grinning, her smile punctuated by shiny silver bridgework.

"Sit down," the Seer said to Soon. "It's been a long time since you've had a rest." She held out her hands for the baby and nodded toward a big chair in the corner, where Soon sat down and, within seconds, fell asleep.

"I suppose you're wondering what's going on," the Seer said to Almost while rocking Never Satisfied—a bit too quickly, Almost thought.

Almost nodded. The Seer picked up a remote control and pointed it at the TV, and suddenly, Almost's parents were there on the screen, younger, as they appeared in the old photos. Vee was obviously pregnant. They were walking with another man down a hallway to a room with a nameplate on the door. The man opened the door and ushered Vee inside what turned out to be a dressing room.

"Please make yourself comfortable," he said to Vee.

"We'll be right back," Almost's father said, and he kissed Vee tenderly.

Once the door closed, Vee was left alone with a poster of the other man, the Great Canterini, which hung on the wall behind the gold brocade sofa where she sat. She dug through her purse, popped a Lifesaver into her mouth, and then fidgeted for a few minutes. Then she rose and made a tour of the room, examining the items laid out in front of the vanity mirror, on the end tables, and on the small desk. She paused at the desk to read the warning pasted to the lid of a lockbox on which the padlock dangled, its shackle unfastened. Her hand reached out and opened the box, and the TV screen cut to black.

"Your mother read the secret to another magician's illusion," the Seer said to Almost. "It's not clear if she meant to do anything with it or if her curiosity just got the best of her. What is clear is that she broke the code magicians are sworn to uphold."

Another scene materialized on the screen, Almost's father arguing with the Great Canterini.

"You can't be serious!" Ever Lilts said, his eyes wide with panic.

"I've never been more serious," the other man said. "Give me your firstborn child or suffer my curse."

"I won't do it!" Almost's father said.

The Great Canterini lifted his hands in a dramatic gesture in front of Ever Lilts's face, spread his fingers wide, and drew his hands apart, as though opening curtains. "Your child will inherit your most precious trait," he said. "As she grows stronger in it, you will grow weaker, until she has siphoned it all away."

"His magic?" Almost asked the Seer, who nodded. "He thought you might have inherited some of it as well," she said, "which is why he kept track of you over the years."

The scene on the TV screen changed again, this time to show Ever Lilts gathering the baby from her bassinet in the dead of night. As he stole down the staircase of the house on Morris Street, Soon followed silently after him. After Almost's father put the baby into the back seat of the car,

Soon, who had realized that something was very wrong with his uncle, snuck in on the other side.

"I drew your father here," the Seer said, "where I could offer some sort of guidance to the children. But the baby was already quite powerful by the time they arrived, and her magic is all over the place. I believe she's the one who has stopped time here in the forest. She took up residence in that tree and wouldn't let any of us pick her up."

"Is there a way to break the curse?" Almost asked.

"Rumor has it, you have everything you need to put things right."

Almost's eyes opened wide. "Me?" she said.

Tab the cat meowed.

"It will come to you," the Seer said. She rose and gave Almost the baby, who had begun to cry again.

Almost rocked her sister. She paced around the small cottage, but the baby continued to cry and twist in her arms. The sound squeezing her heart, Almost went through the kitchen and out the back door into a shriveled garden. She bent her head close to her sister's and began to sing softly, one of the songs on her father's recording. *Red light, green light, round the town.*

The baby stilled, listened.

Found a penny on the ground, Almost sang. *Met a friend I never knowed, walking down old rocky road. Red, green, old rocky road. Tell me what you see.*

She continued to sing as she maneuvered her backpack from her shoulders and pulled out the bag of seeds Therefore had given to her. She sang and jiggled the baby in her arms while she sprinkled seeds over ground hard as stone. As soon as the first seeds touched the earth, the heels of her sandals sank into the dirt. She could feel the trees waking up, the sap softening and beginning to run again. The baby made a sound like *ahhh*.

And as the ground thawed and the buds swelled around her, Almost felt something inside her break open. She gulped and clutched the baby tightly to her chest. *My heart*, she thought.

The baby was growing now at a rapid rate in Almost's arms. She felt the Seer's bony grip on her shoulder and turned to see that the others had joined her and Never in the garden. Soon was at least two inches taller than he had been when Almost first met him.

The Seer took Never from Almost and said, "I have to get them out of the forest now, or they'll be grown before your mother even gets to see them."

Never, propped now on the Seer's hip, stared around the garden, unblinking.

"What about my father?" Almost asked.

They walked around to the front of the cottage and stood over her father's body. His open mouth was full of agates that glistened like spit, and they littered his torso and the path that Almost had made dragging the litter out of the trees.

Why, Almost wondered bitterly, hadn't he confronted Vee about her transgression? Why hadn't he told her about the Great Canterini's curse? Surely there was something they could have done about it together. This man's fear and greed had made him willing to kill his own child. He had stolen Almost's family from her, stolen her life. How happy they had been. Before her. Without her. All these years, her sorrow had gathered and frozen in a solid column in her throat, but now it was melting. Her tears fell for the first time, dropping down onto Mr. Still's body, splashing onto his face and throat like a baptism.

The Seer said that Almost only had to touch his skin with the spots of her mother's blood to reanimate him. But when Almost took out the cloth and unfolded it, the drops of blood spoke to her.

"If you bring him back now," they cried in unison, "you bring back Mr. Still."

Almost imagined returning to her mother's house and revealing Vee's own part in what had happened to her family. She imagined presenting Mr. Still as Vee's long-lost husband. All of that plus the fur coat might just drive her round the bend for good. On the other hand, Almost herself might be able to forge a relationship with her father, regardless. If nothing else, they could go on Dr. Phil: "Daughters Who Kill Their Fathers and Then Bring Them Back to Life."

The Seer interrupted her reverie. "If you want the man your mother fell in love with," she said, "you have to take him down to be judged. We'll meet you at the Airstream."

Then Tab the cat's silver charm winked in the sun, and the group disappeared before Almost's eyes.

XII

HOW MR. STILL GOT A SECOND CHANCE

The Seer's Doberman pinscher walked long-legged out of the cottage, wearing a leather harness. Almost gingerly hitched him to Mr. Still's litter and followed him into the trees. They walked for miles, until they came upon a crude shelter in a stand of pines. Through the beaded curtain that marked the doorway, Almost saw three shrouded figures lounging on a sectional sofa.

"The Seer said you might be willing to hear my case," she said, and the three nodded, one after another.

They listened to her story and then sprang from the couch and swarmed the dead man, tearing him to pieces while

Almost screamed in horror. She saw in her mind's eye the ways Mr. Still had used his paltry remaining magic over the years—to win at dice in bars and at low-stakes blackjack games at the casino in Windsor, to perform the balls and cups for children at birthday parties and bar mitzvahs. She felt the hollow ache where his magic had once been, felt his ruined hope, the rage that brought him back to the woods again and again to try to kill the baby.

When the judges stepped back, two figures—Mr. Still and Mr. Lilts—lay side by side on the damp dirt floor.

"And what about the curse?" she asked the judges.

"The curse has played out," they said, as one. "The magic will find its level now between the father and daughter in a way we cannot predict."

Almost nodded. She took a deep breath and crouched beside her father's body and touched the drops of her mother's blood to his wrists, his temples, and his lips, which parted instantly and sucked in the humid air. One of the judges opened a footlocker and pulled out an Adidas T-shirt, a pair of jeans, and some deck shoes, which they gave to Mr. Lilts, who dressed in a daze. By the time he had tied his shoes, he was conscious enough to recognize Almost. She looked just like her mother, he said. He hugged her tightly, and Almost gasped at the pain in her newly awakened heart.

"Excuse us," the judges said. They explained that they would keep Mr. Still with them, to punish according to his crimes. They had awakened him from death, but only after imprisoning him in a huge sack. Almost could see him struggling inside it like a Houdini escape gone wrong. The judges would send him backward through the phases of life until he reached infancy again. Then they would give the baby to a good home. The judge in the white robe spoke to Almost's father in a high, squeaky voice. "You, too, have a second chance," they said. "Don't blow it."

The judge in the black robe stage-whispered, "And don't visit here again unless you plan to stay. Either of you."

The judge in the gray robe shook back their sleeve and snapped their plump fingers, which resembled two huge maggots, and Almost and her father found themselves at the edge of the forest, outside Tab's trailer.

XIII

HOW THE PROTAGONIST ALMOST
REALIZED HER HEART'S DESIRES

The Seer sat on the tailgate of Tab's truck, clutching a bag of Dunkin' donuts and swinging her feet like a little girl.

"Good, you made it," she said to Almost and her father, flashing her bridgework. "Look." She pointed, and when Almost turned around, she could see that everything in the forest was blooming. The smell of flowering dogwood perfumed the air. The seer shook Almost's and her father's hands and then moved stiffly but steadily into the trees and was gone.

Inside the trailer, Tab had resumed his human form and was playing Go Fish with Soon and Never Satisfied, who was now a little girl. She would grow up at the normal rate now that she was out of the forest, Tab said. Soon, who had aged only a couple of years in his sleep, complained that Never already knew how to cheat. They all laughed, and after Never won the game, they climbed into Tab's truck and drove to Vee's estate.

Almost had never seen her mother cry, and she watched closely as thick tears squeezed out from under Vee's closed eyelids. Vee tried to hold them all close at once—Ever Lilts and Almost, Never Satisfied and Soon, and even Tab.

For supper, the cooks prepared roast chickens and corn on the cob, and Almost invited Therefore the gardener, who brought a bouquet of zinnias for the table. They hugged Almost's father and shook Tab's and Soon's hands and pinched Almost's cheeks, and they and the little girl Never smiled at each other. Tab and Almost held hands under the table during the meal. No one talked yet about what had happened all those years ago. They saved those conversations for the story that would begin the next day. After supper, Almost's father played his guitar, and he and Vee sang the old songs long into the night.

HARMONY OF THE SPHERES

He's been singing since the crib!" Jimmy's mother had told the interviewer from *People*, which showed Jimmy on the cover in leather pants with the caption "Jimmy Jams!"

Daniel could not bring himself to listen to the recordings. He remembered too clearly the nights in the bedroom they had shared as boys, when Jimmy played the same song endlessly on his guitar, when he would not stop singing, though Daniel shouted and begged and tore at his ears like a madman.

Everything was a song to Jimmy. Basketball. Mowing the lawn. Taking a crap. Sounds began in his stomach, he told Daniel in a ghost-story voice, then rose up through his throat and out his mouth involuntarily.

One night, Daniel leaned out of bed, plucked his telescope from its stand, and bashed Jimmy with it. He watched Jimmy's silhouette on the wall, his shadow hands rising to clutch his shadow face. Then Jimmy began to scream melodically, and the light burst on.

"Dammit, Daniel!" their mother yelled from the doorway.

The telescope had split Jimmy's lip, exploding blood over his face and Partridge Family pajamas.

Though Daniel was ashamed to admit it aloud, he revisited that scene often throughout his lifetime—while staring through the glass roof of the observatory where he worked, for instance, or lying next to his sleeping wife—relishing those precious moments between the blow and Jimmy's cries, that interlude during which he had first sensed the vast, silent workings of the universe.

THIS IS YOUR LIFE

The Sixties

How about it? Pastor Joe asks. He wants you and your wife to run the youth group at Good Shepherd this year. Sipping his coffee, he pins your wife to her chair with his good eye while the other drifts, moving as though he is tracking of the rest of the congregation milling around the church basement. And that's how you end up spending Saturday afternoons playing guitar and singing folk songs, talking about the war and listening to a bunch of teenagers complain about their parents and school, things you always hated too.

One of the girls has long blond hair that falls down to where her heart-shaped ass curves out from her body. She is sixteen but looks nineteen. You see her at a bar one night. Shhh, she says, don't tell anyone the truth about me. She bums your cigarettes and persuades you to buy her a couple of beers. An hour later, the two of you are out in your car in the alley smoking a joint, and one thing leads to another.

Her mother approaches you after church one Sunday. Your heart is suddenly struggling, jumping against your chest like the grasshoppers you used to catch in your hands as a boy.

But you listen and nod as she explains that her daughter has become more withdrawn lately and has been coming home reeking of smoke and liquor. Would it be possible at the youth group meetings to talk about the dangers of drugs with the kids? She asks it almost shyly, and you see the shadow of her daughter in the way she looks up at you without lifting her head, the way her fingers brush her gray-streaked hair back behind one ear.

The girl comes to the youth group meetings a few more times, sporadically, and when she's there, it makes you uncomfortable. She's always staring at you, at your hand on your wife's shoulder. When she stops coming altogether, you are secretly relieved. Your wife tries to call her, to find out what went wrong. The other kids say they haven't seen her. You worry for a few months that the girl might tell somebody what happened between you. You think about her at the factory where you work filling molds with plastic foam. Having something to think about makes the shifts go by faster.

The Seventies

A stripper with incredible tits. A waitress who thinks you're the funniest guy *ever*. The manager's girlfriend. A friend's wife. The other married woman with the horses. A drug addict you meet at the unemployment office. Your boss's daughter. A college girl. A stranger.

The Eighties

At home after the bar closes, you leave a note for your wife: *I'll be playing poker all night. See you tomorrow. Love you.*

Later you wonder what gave you away, if, as she read the words you'd written, small details from the past came together in her head like the colored pieces in a kaleidoscope falling into a pattern that actually looked like something—a flower or the shape of a face. Instead of going to work in the morning, your wife shows up on your girlfriend's front step. Her banging on the screen door reminds you of your kids when they were young, how nearly every Saturday morning they would start you out of a sound sleep by banging their toys around or yelling at each other or turning the TV up too loud.

At the door, you try to explain to your wife that you were just helping out a friend, that you slept on the couch. As you tell the story, you become convinced that it is true, that if you turned around just now and looked at the couch, there would be a blanket there, a pillow with a dent in it where your head had been. But she won't buy it. In her rage, her lips are so thin they've nearly disappeared. You can't help staring at the place where her lips used to be. Get your shit from the house, she says. Then get out.

The Nineties

Two straight days of cocaine, whiskey, and poker. The sun has been up for hours when you finally get back to your girlfriend's apartment. The bedroom stinks of farts and sweat and sex. You take off your clothes and lie in the stinking bed for a long time with your eyes closed, your eyeballs jerking around under the lids, thinking about all the things you don't want to think about: how you only have five dollars left from your unemployment check, how that means you'll have to ask your girlfriend for money again, how you owe child support for your sons—your ex-wife says that proves you don't care at all, as if money is everything.

Finally you drift off, but only minutes later your girl-friend's daughter comes home from school, turns the TV on, and starts rattling dishes around in the kitchen. Your eyes flip open; your blood surges. Shut up! you yell from the bed, but either she doesn't hear you, or she is ignoring you. You fling open the bedroom door and stand there in your underwear. An unkind breeze blows against your growing paunch. She is at the sink with her back to you. Shut up! you shout again. I'm trying to sleep in here!

Fuck you, she says without turning around. You don't even pay rent here.

She is thirteen, the undisciplined child of a slut. The surprise on her face when you are suddenly next to her at the sink gives your anger an edge of pleasure. You slap her across the head and push her into the counter when she tries to turn away. When she falls down onto the vinyl flooring, you start to kick her—in the ass, in the bare places where her cropped shirt has crawled up and the wavy pattern of ribs presses up against her skin. She screams, the television blares, and then someone is knocking on the door. It's the neighbor, wondering if everything is okay. Though you assure her that it is, she still calls the police.

Your girlfriend presses charges against you, not because she wants to, she says, but because the social worker told her it's the right thing to do if she wants to keep her kid. The judge who issues the restraining order strongly suggests you get out of town. You call a guy you know in Rochester. Last time you saw him, he said he needed a blacktopper.

The Nineties, Part Two

You are pleasantly surprised when your ex-girlfriend calls and asks you to drive over from Rochester to have dinner with her, just for old times' sake. Why not? you say. A guy named Jake is living with her now. She asks if you're sure you're not jealous. No, you tell her. After hanging up the phone, you wonder about it for a moment. You don't remember ever having felt something you'd call jealousy. You search your body to see if it knows what the word might mean, and it answers with a deep blankness, a rhythmic silence. Then your back twinges where you strained a muscle looking over your shoulder while backing the steamroller over a newly asphalted parking lot.

When you and your ex meet, it's like old times—without having to go home to an apartment that smells like an ashtray and where the bathroom is always covered with a gray layer of filth. You splurge on an expensive restaurant, where the steaks are tender and bloody. You are on your second bottle of wine by the time you get to the cheesecake.

You're both drunk and laughing when you leave. It must be below zero outside, but the cold air feels good on your face and neck. Tiny snowflakes fall like glitter from the sky, which, as you stand under a streetlight looking up, seems very far away. Before you get into the car, your ex throws her arms around your neck and kisses you. What about Jake? you ask. She says, It's Jack, and he's working the overnight shift.

On your way back to her apartment, a big old Buick flies through a stop sign, and you can't keep your Datsun from hitting it broadside at thirty miles an hour. The sound is enormous, a rough chord of brakes and metal bending. The back window on the Buick gives and sends a shower of glass over the hood of your car.

You sit in the steaming silence, your right ankle throbbing, your ex-girlfriend's arm limp across your lap. Then the other driver is yelling, My God, I'm sorry, my brakes, is everyone okay? People come out of the bar on the corner. Your ex is hunched over the stick shift, her face turned toward you.

She is snoring softly, and a thin red line runs from her nose, which might have broken when she hit the windshield. She'll be really pissed if it mars her good looks. Gently, you push her back into her seat and lean her head against the window.

There is a hospital just a few blocks away, and the ambulance arrives almost immediately. The paramedics lay your ex gently on the stretcher and roll her away.

Before you can get out of the car, the cop on the scene saunters over to take your statement. Hey, look who it is! the cop says while shining his flashlight into your car, the beam sweeping over the empty beer cans in your back seat.

Jerry! you say. How are you, man?

You went to high school with Jerry. He was a jock but was nice to everyone.

Wow, you say. Believe it or not, I was just thinking about you the other night watching the Bucks. That last-second basket you made that took us to the championship—that was some basket.

Jerry the jock laughs with obvious pleasure, the hometown hero, and you are pleased to see that he is pleased to see you, to be recognized by you.

How have you been? Jerry asks. Not having such a great night, I see.

You're not kidding! you say.

That your wife they took to the ER?

Ex-girlfriend, you say gingerly, raising an eyebrow.

Ouch! Jerry the jock winces, and the two of you laugh together.

This obviously wasn't your fault, Jerry says. He leans in, says confidentially, I don't want to get the Breathalyzer out.

No, no, you say. Appreciate that.

So, tell you what, why don't you go wait inside the bar, where it's warm, and I'll have the bartender call you a cab.

He hands you his card with the other driver's insurance information written on the back.

You have some difficulty getting out of driver's seat, and Jerry asks if you need medical attention.

No, no, you say, putting some weight on your right ankle, which at least is not broken. Then, feeling like one lucky son of a bitch, you hobble into the bar, where the bartender not only calls you a cab but also gives you a free draft while you wait. You describe the accident for her—the slow-motion crumpling of the front end of your car, your ex flopping around like a giant doll. In no time, the cab is honking outside.

A thin layer of snow has dusted the cars parked up and down the block. The cabbie has his window down and is puffing on a cigarette. It's Richie, a guy you were friends with back in the seventies, when you were bartending at a strip joint on the other side of town. He used to bring his wife to the bar. The two of them would have a couple of beers, watch the girls dance for a little while, then go home. The strippers were like foreplay to them. One night Richie's wife showed up without him. She was crying and said they'd had a fight. You took her upstairs to the office to try to calm her down, and one thing led to another. She ended up straddling you on the swivel office chair, pumping until you thought the big spring under the seat would break. You don't know if she told Richie about it that night to get back at him, or if she'd told him later, out of guilt. Either way, Richie had never talked to you again. You heard that he and his wife started going over to the Yum Yum Tree after that.

When Richie sees you walking toward his cab, he gives you the finger and speeds away, fishtailing down the block. Fuck you, too, Richie! you shout after him, but you find it hard to blame him. Your ankle still hurts as though some big fist is squeezing and twisting it, but you decide to walk the six blocks to the emergency room anyway. Your ex-girlfriend is most likely conscious by now, and without a car to get back to Rochester, you'll need a place to stay. Maybe you can sleep in her hospital room and figure out what to do in the morning.

As you limp along the sidewalk, the snowflakes so gentle and cold on your face, you see that the evening has been all about the past—being on a date with your ex and then running into not only Jerry but also Richie. It reminds you of the TV show you used to watch as a kid, where, after a lot of fanfare, the host would bring out the guest's best friend from grade school, his favorite teacher, people he'd almost forgotten but whose lives had touched his in the small ways that added up to something. You wonder who else the producers might dig up if you were the guest star. The man who sold you your first joint? Your father, back from the grave, lamenting how you'd never lived up to the hopes he had for you? You smile imagining the long line of women waiting backstage. Some of them you wouldn't mind seeing again.

THE BLACK CAR

Standing in the driveway, Michael sees his own thin stupid face reflected in the black car's glossy flank. He sees that he has become even smaller, that he is now suspended in darkness. His real mother gave him up because he was sickly. Is that why his foster parents are sending him away? Or is it simply that they like her better—the soft rosy girl who now sleeps in the other twin bed in his room and who chatters happily over her breakfast?

Michael climbs into the back seat and pulls the heavy door closed, but it only clicks half-heartedly. When the lanky new father gets in behind the wheel, Michael thinks of a folding ruler or a marionette. There is something wooden about him, the thin grayish hair brushed flat across his head as though painted on.

The car backs out of the driveway, and the motion tips Michael against the door—which opens as the car accelerates down the street, and Michael spills out. The world goes topsy-turvy, a kaleidoscope of blue sky, black branches, orange leaves. Then jarring pain in his shoulder and head, and his nose and mouth fill with the smells of asphalt and gasoline, the rot of wet leaves in the gutter.

Is it his body screaming? No, the sound is coming from the adults' gaping mouths as they run toward him. He cringes, terrified by the sound, but his foster mother reaches him first, and his fingers grip the sleeve of the soft periwinkle cardigan she wears this time of year. His longing for her eclipses the throb in his head, the burning in his arm.

Then the new father steps between them. His long wooden fingers grasp Michael's upper arms and lift him carefully to his feet, brush the leaves from his pants. The black car crouches in the middle of the street, three of its doors open like tongues lolling, as if it has spit him out. Even the beast has found him distasteful.

The new mother bends to squint at Michael. He doesn't know yet that this squint is her permanent expression. She has a twitchy face, eyes that reflect the light wrong. Large pores on an upturned nose. Flaking coral lipstick and brown-painted eyebrows.

Did you open that door?

Her voice floods Michael with shame, even though he didn't do it. His eyes well up, and a scoffing sound scrapes up out of the new mother's throat, as if something is scrabbling in there, trying to get out.

Did you?

The shame filters down inside him, mixes with grief and the love he has known in his short life, and a voice inside him speaks for the first time: *No!* it says aloud, indignant.

The new father pats Michael's body clumsily. *You're all right*, he says gruffly.

He carries Michael like a baby back to the car and closes the door firmly this time, so that the air inside boxes Michael's ears.

As the car roars away from the only family he remembers, away from his home, his street, his neighborhood, the voice speaks, silently this time—*No!*—and he feels the revving of an unfamiliar power.

No! the voice shouts later, when the new mother wrestles him into the laundry hamper and sits on top of it, breathing heavily for fear of the devil she says lives inside him. Hunched there in the dark, looking out through the cracks between the woven strands of wicker, it is clear to Michael where the devil is.

No! the voice says, furiously, when the puppet-father doesn't listen, leaves him alone with the mother, day after day.

The voice makes him someone unexpected. It sharpens his mind, hardens his muscles, adds inches to his height and words to his vocabulary. The children he works with after earning his PhD trust him instinctively, as though they have access to the scene that reels out in his mind again and again, the scene that changes over time until the black car coughs him out into the moldy mush of leaves, and he finally understands what it is telling him.

This time he springs up and runs like hell.

PEG'S CAT

Amber wore a lemon-yellow pantsuit her first day at University Student Services. On her way to Mr. Leeds's office, she smiled nervously at the packs of high-heeled women standing around desks and coffee makers and in the doorways of offices and cubicles, and they smiled back at her without revealing their teeth. Their whispering stopped when she approached and then began again as she passed, a sound like the wind through the trees that lined the streets on campus.

It took Mr. Leeds two hours to introduce her to everyone. Each time they approached a new "team," he had to find out how everyone's weekend had gone and then describe the barbeque he had attended on Saturday.

"Have you had a bratwurst yet this summer?" Mr. Leeds said to each team, although they had likely heard him say it to the previous team on the other side of the cubicle wall. "Well, I suggest you do!" He laughed merrily, and everyone laughed along with him, like the laugh track on a sitcom.

Amber was exhausted by the time he led her to a room across the hall from his office. Inside, a woman sat with her back to the door.

"You'll share your space with Peg, my other assistant," Mr. Leeds said.

Peg swung around in her chair. Her feet dangled several inches above the carpet, and under a bush of wiry gray-brown hair, her forehead slumped onto the bridge of her bulbous nose. Small eyes peered out from the caves formed by her brows and fleshy cheeks. She smiled, and her full purplish lips pulled back to reveal small gapped teeth. She was wearing a red and purple plaid polyester blazer.

"Nice to meet you, Amber," she said in a throaty voice and held out a hand the size of a baseball glove. Amber's slender fingers disappeared for a moment in her grasp.

Mr. Leeds pulled a chair up to Amber's desk and began to explain her daily duties. Amber sat next to him and nodded and stifled yawns as he expounded on long-distance fax codes and Windows, how he couldn't believe he had forgotten to tell everyone that at the barbeque his dog had jumped into the pool, the password for this, the code for that, Excel something-or-other, blah, blah, blah.

When he finally left Amber alone, it was lunchtime. She eased back in her ergonomic chair and smoothed the lap of her yellow pants. The door to the office was open, and beyond it, she could hear a woman's voice whispering, but no matter how hard she concentrated, she couldn't catch a word of it. She squinted at the dark computer screen. She didn't even remember how to turn it on.

"Hi, Amber! How's it going so far?"

Amber swiveled toward the door and saw a perky dark-haired woman leaning in the doorway. She couldn't remember the woman's name or what team she was on.

"Mr. Leeds just left," Amber said, "so I haven't really—"

"It'll be a breeze." The woman lifted her chin and shook her head as if to shake back her hair, only her chin-length bob didn't move at all. "Say," the woman said, "I don't know if anyone mentioned this, but the last person in this position was a real piece of work. She could not tell her head from her hinder, if you know what I mean, and because she was so, well, how should I say it, incompetent, Leeds pawned off some of her work on me—just the mailing list for alumni surveys, no big deal—so I was thinking since you seem like a capable gal, I'd just bring that over, show you the database, and you could take that over again, since it is in your job description."

"Well," Amber said, "if it's in my job description."

"Great!" the perky woman said. As she turned to leave, she nearly ran into Peg, who was returning from the bathroom.

"What evil mission are you on, Jean?" Peg growled. "Trying to dump your work on unsuspecting newbies again?"

Jean fake-laughed. "Oh, Peg, you're such a card," she said and walked away.

Peg raised a shaggy eyebrow at Amber. "I hope you said no. These bitches'll get you coming and going unless you learn to say no."

Amber chewed her upper lip. What had she been thinking taking this job and then charging five hundred dollars' worth of clothes on her Visa? When Mr. Leeds had called to offer her the position, she'd felt only a slight twinge of guilt accepting it. Sure she'd doctored her résumé a little, but she was sick of waiting tables at Lance's Kitchen, kissing up to the cranky regulars to try to make up in tips for the crappy wage. And the cute cook, Barry, had dumped her for the new hostess, making every day a new adventure in humiliation. Mr. Leeds obviously hadn't checked all her references, since the second and third ones were completely made up. The office job paid double what she made as a waitress, plus benefits, and, really, how difficult could office work be?

Now she stared at the stacks of tapes for transcription, data to be entered, and papers to be prioritized, copied, sorted, and filed. She wished she hadn't said she could type fifty words a minute when it was really more like twenty-five—while looking at the keys. A feeling of panic rose into her chest like heartburn. She hunched over her desk and began to weep quietly, and when a stream of snot began running from her nose, she used the heel of one hand to stem it.

Peg rose and closed the office door. "There, there," she said. She offered Amber some tissues and then patted her on the shoulder with one huge hand. "We'll get it done."

Amber's tears ceased abruptly. "We will?" she asked. "But how?"

"I'll help you," Peg said. "But first, why don't you run down and see if there are any of those nice pastries left in the cafeteria."

Amber raced downstairs and returned with two apricot Danish, which Peg gobbled down, scattering crumbs all over her chest and stomach. She burped softly and with her plump pinkie wiped blobs of icing from the corners of her mouth. She unfastened the gold plastic buttons on her blazer.

"Bring me that stack of tapes," she said, pointing. "You can answer the phones while I type."

"East Central Illinois University Undergraduate Student Services Center office," Amber sang into the phone all day with a forced enthusiasm that made her head ache. "This is Amber speaking. How may I help you?"

She had some trouble transferring people properly, and once, a man interrupted her by saying, "Yeah, yeah, I heard it before, babe. Gimme Dean White." But Amber chewed her lip and forged on, spurred by the sound of Peg's furious typing. By four thirty, her throat ached, but her desk was clear. What truly amazed her was that Peg's own desk was also empty of work.

At four thirty, Mr. Leeds checked in on Amber.

"My God," he said, leafing through a file folder stuffed with what was supposedly Amber's transcription. "It's unbelievable!"

Amber blushed.

The next day, Amber wore a spring-green skirt-and-vest ensemble that accented the red highlights in her dark blond hair. After stopping to chat with Jean in Records, she entered her office, only to find her desk piled even higher than the previous day. Mr. Leeds stuck his head in.

"I hope you don't mind, Amber," he said, pushing his glasses up the bridge of his nose. "Dr. Boone's secretary is out today, and he needs those orientation materials copied, those tapes transcribed, and that booklet proofread, copied, and bound. The spiral binder is out here near the mailboxes."

Amber nodded vaguely.

"Attagirl!" Mr. Leeds gave her a thumbs-up.

Once he was gone, Amber closed the door and burst into tears. Hadn't she loved the greasy-grill smell of Lance's Kitchen? Hadn't she been secretly flattered when the per-verted bartender's arm "accidentally" brushed against her breasts? She felt pricks of grateful love in her heart just thinking about the overweight local businessmen who had come in every Monday and Wednesday for lunch, slaves to her fake smile.

Amber's crying intensified when the door opened and Peg appeared wearing orange polyester pants and a puffy-sleeved floral smock. Peg stroked Amber's naturally wavy hair with one of her big mitts.

"Don't cry, Amber," Peg crooned. "Peg's here. Peg's your friend."

"There's no way I could get even half of this done today," Amber said in a small voice, "even if I was a good secretary like you."

"You poor kid." Peg smashed Amber's head to her chest. "Shhh," she whispered close to Amber's ear. Her breath smelled like Band-Aids. "I'll help you."

"I don't know how to thank you, Peg."

Wasn't it just an expression? Something a person said when she was feeling grateful? Amber hadn't really meant that she was looking for a way to thank Peg, but when she said it, Peg stepped back and eyed her in a wistful way.

"Well, there is one thing," she said.

Amber's stomach clenched a little.

"You could call me later, after supper, to keep me company. And maybe we could go out to eat together sometime after work. I get so lonely at night, what with the kids gone and all. My neighbors are useless. The lady on the one side is so old, it takes her all day to get out of bed and most of the night to get back in, and the couple on the other side doesn't get home until nine thirty at night, and my friend Elizabeth used to live across the—"

"All right!" Amber agreed brightly, although she was beginning to think just being stuck in the office with Peg was a pretty fair trade, what with her answering the phones and beautifying the place and all.

That evening, Amber stalled as long as she could. She ate her Lean Cuisine pasta primavera so slowly that it was cold before she finished. She watched an old rerun of *Friends* then read *Glamour* while soaking in the tub. Finally, she picked up the phone to call Peg, although her throat was still sore from work. It hardly mattered, she soon discovered, since Peg yakked nonstop. She apparently had been dying to tell Amber about how her marriage had fallen apart and how her grown kids never called.

Peg talked with her lips pressed against the mouthpiece of the phone, making her frequent sighs so loud that Amber was forced to yank the receiver away from her ear. "But I don't really miss him," Peg said. "Except for the sex."

Amber gagged silently.

The next morning, Dean Boone's petite blond secretary, Debbie, stopped by Amber's desk to thank her for covering the day before.

"No problem," Amber said weakly.

"Do you want to have lunch with me and some of the other girls today?" Debbie asked.

"Sure!" Amber said.

"Anything to escape the troll's clutches, right?" Debbie leaned across Amber's desk in a way that made her blouse part, and Amber glimpsed her breasts overflowing from a tiny black bra.

"Good morning, Amber," Peg said from the doorway. "Debbie. You're looking like a streetwalker this morning, as usual. I think I hear Dean Boone clamoring for his morning blow job."

Debbie's mouth opened wide, but no sound came out, and she huffed silently out of the office. The whispering just beyond the doorway seemed to rise in Debbie's wake and then die down again as Peg took off her windbreaker and hung it on the coat-tree. She settled into her chair and grinned at Amber over the mounds of work that had appeared on their desks overnight.

"Ready?" she said, and Amber couldn't help but smile back at her.

"Ready," she said.

Weeks passed, and soon Amber had finished her three-month probation and was awarded a raise. She got a letter of special recognition from Dean Boone for a grant proposal she had supposedly written for his office. And two evenings a week, she dialed Peg's number and mumbled "Uh huh" and "Really" at what seemed appropriate times, reading magazines or watching television as Peg rambled on.

One Tuesday morning shortly after Amber's six-month anniversary at Student Services, Mr. Leeds asked her to come into his office and close the door. He had been very friendly toward Amber since she'd started working for him, and they'd lunched together several times, but she'd kept a certain distance, lest he discover her true incompetence. Not to mention that his head was too big for his thin body and that from the back he looked like a frail old man in his baggy dress pants.

In all honesty, she had her eye on the tall brown-eyed Dean Boone, Debbie's boss. She just hadn't been able to get away from her office long enough to even flirt with him yet.

"Most of us have done him already," Debbie had said when Amber mentioned him over lunch, "and I'm sure his wife appreciates not getting poked in the back every night."

The other girls had tittered.

"Amber," Byron Leeds said to her that morning. "It's been a pleasure getting to know you. Maybe I flatter myself to think that the special appreciation I feel for you is mutual, but I'm going to go out on a limb here. Would you like to have dinner with me?"

"I would enjoy that, Byron, very much," Amber said softly, hoping her shy sincerity seemed genuine.

Mr. Leeds clapped his hands like a boy at his own birthday party. Then he sobered. "As I'm sure you know," he said, "Part five, section C of the employee handbook states that it is against policy for a supervisor to fraternize with his employees."

Amber nodded as though she knew what the word *fraternize* meant while Byron fingered his thin lower lip. He leaned toward her conspiratorially. "What I'd like to propose is a little risqué," he continued. "I have a friend in the engineering department who has informed me that they need a new receptionist. If you transfer to that position, the pay scale will be the same."

Transfer? Receptionist? Amber knew how to greet people. She knew how to answer a telephone. And Peg had even shown her how to turn on a computer.

"I am worried about one thing," Byron said. "They don't have half the work in a week in engineering that we get here every day. I'm afraid you might be terribly bored."

"Hmm." Amber pretended to weigh her options. She might even sleep with Byron for this. "I guess we all have to make sacrifices," she said, "when we want something badly enough." It was a line she might have gleaned from an old episode of *Little House on the Prairie*, and it seemed to please Byron, who got busy filling out the paperwork for her transfer. In less than two weeks, she would begin her new job.

She left Byron's office and met the girls in the back corner of the cafeteria, where they were plotting to find out what size pants the Social Activities intern really wore. Gail from Social Activities, who had straight black hair and a permanent suntan like Elizabeth Taylor in *Cleopatra*, imitated the intern in a Minnie Mouse voice. "I love Banana Republic," she said, "because I can wear a six there when I wear an eight everywhere else."

"If she wears an eight in any brand," Debbie said grimly, "I'll fuck my husband twice tonight."

"Tell you what," Jean said, "next time she goes to the bathroom, I'll burst into her stall and see what I can see."

"You might need help," Gail said. "I'll buzz you and Debbie on the intercom when she heads for the bathroom, then meet you there." She tossed her black hair over her shoulder and eyed Amber. "You in?"

Amber smiled uncertainly. Sure, she and the other waitresses at Lance's had spit in the drinks and food of certain customers who had treated them badly, and sure, they complained behind each other's backs and even conspired sometimes to get someone fired, but Amber had never seen anything like what went on in Student Services. The good secretaries sabotaged the better ones, the Admissions staff told Financial Aid jokes, Career Services undermined Undergraduate Advising, and Byron Leeds and the deans floated above it all, oblivious of the jockeying in the lower ranks. At the bottom of the hierarchy were the students, who were universally hated. The Social Activities intern was a student in the Department of Recreation and Physical Education.

Amber reconsidered sharing the news of her transfer with the girls. If they thought Byron had done her a special favor, they might rip her to pieces.

"Well?" Debbie said. They were all staring at her.

"Sure," Amber said. "I'm in."

By the time Amber got back to her office, she was bursting from holding her good news in for so long. She should have known better than to tell Peg about it, though. The short woman was furious.

"What am I supposed to do, Peg," Amber finally asked, desperate to quell Peg's throaty ranting about loyalty and friendship, "give up a job I might really be able to do just so you won't be lonely?"

Peg sputtered.

"I won't give up the job, Peg," Amber said.

"Then I'll have to tell them the truth about you!" Peg's voice became uncharacteristically high and thin. "I'll even tell Byron you pick your nose and wipe it under the desk."

Amber's blood sank and pooled suddenly in her feet, making her lightheaded. She put her head between her knees. She'd thought Peg was too busy to notice the nasty habit that had carried over from childhood.

"Just because I'll be over in engineering doesn't mean we won't still be friends," Amber said, her voice muffled by her lavender linen skirt. "I'll still call you."

But Peg ignored her. Amber had to copy a whole packet of orientation materials by herself that afternoon, and the Xerox machine kept jamming. Peg didn't even turn around when Amber invited her along to the bathroom when Gail called. As Amber, Debbie, and Gail stood at the sinks pretending to wash their hands, the intern ran from the bathroom sobbing and clutching her unfastened khakis while Jean screamed after her, "Size twelve! I knew it! You wear a twelve, fat ass!"

Peg continued to give Amber the silent treatment and play solitaire on her computer for the rest of the day. Amber thought hard but unsuccessfully about how to keep Peg working on her behalf until she left for engineering, how to keep her from blabbing to Byron—although Byron might not even believe a word of it.

"To put it bluntly," he'd told Amber when they were chatting one day in his office after lunch, "I find Peg an extremely unattractive person. In a word, Peg has a bad attitude."

"Has she done something wrong?" Amber had asked, digging for something Peg might have neglected to tell her, a detail that might come in handy should she ever need some leverage.

Byron picked up a pen from his blotter and tapped his chin with it, an annoying habit that, when he held the pen point up as he did now, resulted in a sparse black beard of staccato ink marks on his clean-shaven skin. She wondered how many times a week he had to shave.

"Curiously," he said, "I can't think of anything specific she's done wrong. No one's ever complained directly about her, and I've never caught her in a lie exactly, but she goes through another office mate about every six months. I get the feeling she's always up to something, but I never can figure out what it is."

"But she does good work, right?" Amber prodded. Strangely, the more Byron insulted Peg, the more defensive Amber felt. After all, wasn't Peg's work Amber's work? "I mean, she's so organized, and her transcription's great, and she knows all the computer programs backward and—"

"I've never had any major complaints about her work."

"Is it as good as mine?"

"Doesn't come close." Byron smiled at her across his desk. He looked hungry, although they'd just returned from the cafeteria—in fact, he had a piece of dark green lettuce stuck between his two front teeth.

Remembering how Byron had insulted Peg, Amber decided not to sleep with him after all. Once she transferred to engineering, she would phase both him and Peg out of her life. She would forget she'd ever set foot in Student Services.

The next morning, Peg seemed much calmer.

"I've been thinking about our little arrangement, Amber," she said, "and I'm prepared to offer you a deal. I'll continue to do your work, no strings attached, if you can do one thing."

Amber's heart pounded painfully. Was she prepared to indulge the little troll's perverted sexual fantasies? The yogurt she'd had for breakfast flipped around in her stomach like clothes in a dryer.

"Okay," she said thickly.

"Tell me my cat's name."

"What?"

"It should be easy, Amber," Peg said. "We're friends, right? Surely I've mentioned my cat's name several times during our phone calls."

"I'm not sure you have, Peg, honestly," Amber said, feigning innocence.

"You have three chances to guess my cat's name," Peg said. "For three nights, we'll dine together, and you'll guess. If you guess correctly, I'll do your work without a peep and then disappear from your life when you leave Student Services as though we've never met."

"What if I can't guess it?"

"Then we'll have dinner together once a month, talk on the phone weekly, and you'll join my bowling team."

"What?"

"We're actually very good. Is it a deal?"

"Is the cat a boy or a girl?"

"That's cheating."

Amber racked her brain. Peg's workstation contained several photos of the cat sitting next to the Christmas tree and lolling about on a sheepskin rug. It had long white hair, a pushed-in face, and bottle-green eyes. Peg talked about it frequently, its special diet and how when it was sick with kidney stones it had urinated all over the house. If only Amber had been listening more carefully, she might know the answer to Peg's question right now.

"Fine, it's a deal," Amber said curtly.

"Tonight you're taking me to Lance's Kitchen."

"Oh, Peg, that place holds nothing but bad memories for me. To go back there would be like begging or something."

There wasn't a speck of truth in it—Amber had gone back to Lance's often to have a beer with the girls and flirt with Barry, even though he had dumped her. But she didn't want to be seen there, or anywhere in public, with Peg.

"How about the Olive Garden?" Amber suggested. It was on the outskirts of town and sure to be deserted on a weeknight.

"Lance's Kitchen or no deal," Peg said, swinging around in her chair to face her computer. "Pick me up at seven."

That evening Peg wore a white blouse with a ruffle at the neck and a black spandex mini skirt that made her lumpy hips look like a half-empty tube of toothpaste. The hostess at Lance's, who was still wearing too much bronzer, greeted Amber enthusiastically and gave them the quietest booth. But then she and their waitress—whose skirt length emphasized her thick calves—and the bartender stood at the bar whispering. Barry the cook came through the swinging doors from the kitchen, wiping his hands on his apron. Someone must have tipped him off about the troll Amber had brought to dinner.

Peg downed two cocktails before they'd even ordered their meals, and when she couldn't decide between two entrées, she ordered both and then set upon the food like a starved animal. Amber only picked at her taco salad. She could never come back here again, thanks to Peg, who was now ordering coffee and dessert.

"Oh, my goodness," Peg said fifteen minutes later, leaning over to lick the edge of the tulip glass that had held her hot fudge sundae. "I'm stuffed."

The brown and gray hair framing her face was flecked with Alfredo sauce, one eyebrow was smeared with gravy, and she had a fudgy ring around her mouth.

Fighting back angry tears, Amber left three twenties on the table and pulled Peg out the back door by one of her thick arms. As Amber drove, Peg reclined in the passenger seat, moaning about how much her stomach hurt. Then she sat up and began to spit—great, wet gobs of saliva on the dashboard, the floor, the passenger window. Amber shrieked as a blob of spit landed on the back of her right hand, and she pulled over to the side of the road just in time for Peg to open the door and vomit for an impossibly long time onto the gravel shoulder, making a sound like a garbage disposal. Amber hadn't heard anything like it since she'd dated an alcoholic who threw up first thing every morning.

It was cold outside, but when it seemed Peg was finally finished, she still hung on the car door, panting, her stout body half in, half out of the car. Her skirt had ridden up so that Amber could see most of her cheesy left thigh. She considered putting a foot on one of Peg's haunches, launching her out the door, and driving away. But she still needed her, at least until next week, when Amber would be "training" her own replacement.

"Are you finished?" Amber could not say it nicely.

Peg struggled to get back into the car, but her short limbs and top-heaviness worked against her. Amber grasped Peg's sleeve and pulled her back into the bucket seat, a move she regretted as soon as she saw the vomit-drool hanging from Peg's chin and the ends of her hair, pooled in the ruffles of her blouse. She smelled like meat kept in the refrigerator past its expiration date.

"You could have held my hair back, Amber," Peg sobbed. "I'm starting to think you don't have any human feelings at all."

Amber clenched her teeth. "There now," she said, patting Peg a little too hard on the shoulder, squinting in the dim interior light to make sure she wasn't aiming for a stray patch of vomit. "Let's get you home."

Finally Amber pulled into Peg's driveway.

"Help me inside, won't you, Amber?"

Amber guided Peg into the house. When Peg turned on the lights in the living room, Amber was taken aback. Brilliant rugs in deep reds and purples set off the glowing wood floors. Built-in shelves jumbled with books and framed photographs flanked a broad fireplace. In comparison, Amber's apartment was a dump. With her next check, Amber decided she would buy some new curtains, maybe a matching cover for her couch. She would call maintenance tomorrow about the plaster flaking off the walls in her bathroom.

"You have a lovely home," Amber said.

"You sound surprised," Peg growled, and Amber looked toward the sound, alarmed. Peg had entered the dark corridor and become a shadowy figure with hair hanging over her face, her hands balled into fists. Amber shivered. Then Peg turned and staggered into a room.

Amber thought quickly. Where might she find information about Peg's cat? She looked through the basket of mail next to the telephone, through the papers on the desk, hoping to find a bill from the veterinarian. From the bookshelf she took down a photo of the cat and slid the backing from the frame, but the reverse side revealed only a date.

The other photos on the shelves showed normal-looking people, a short man, a boy, and a girl whom Amber guessed were Peg's former husband and their children. There were graduation pictures of the kids, who had turned out only slightly ugly, although the girl had Peg's unfortunate doorknob of a nose.

In a small brass frame, Amber found a black-and-white photo of a girl in a leotard and tutu, her arms raised to form a graceful circle. It had to be Peg—there was no mistaking the gapped front teeth, the widely spaced eyes—but she actually looked like a little girl a mother could have loved.

Amber stared at the photo for several minutes, lamenting the fact that she, too, would become older and uglier. She turned away and wandered into the kitchen, which was spacious and bright, with teal valances and white wallpaper dotted with tiny teal and yellow flowers. She opened a couple of drawers but found no papers, no clues as to the cat's name. She ran her hands over Peg's stainless-steel range, the stone countertops, the wooden cabinets that felt like satin under her fingertips. Out the kitchen window, she could see a snow-covered sundeck, and she imagined it in the summer furnished with puffy floral chairs and a gas grill.

Amber jumped when something brushed against her leg. It was Peg's cat, looking up at her with wide green eyes. From its green collar, a silver tag dangled.

"Pretty kitty," Amber cooed, rubbing the cat's head with her fingertips. She didn't like cats, or animals in general, and so she was surprised by how good it felt to stroke the silky white fur. "What's your name, kitty?"

The cat began to purr loudly as Amber scratched around its collar, her fingers moving slowly toward the tag under its chin. But just as she was reaching for it, the cat ducked its head and flopped down onto its side on the floor. Amber crouched and stroked the cat's back with her left hand while her right found the tag. She grasped the cool metal chip and turned it over.

In a flash, the cat clutched Amber's wrist with its front claws and bit her hard in the meaty place under her thumb. Panicked, Amber shook her arm violently until the cat fell away. She stood and took a quick step back from the cat, which crouched on the floor in front of her now, its ears flattened. A little blood oozed from the marks on Amber's hand and wrist, less than she expected from how much they hurt. She stepped toward the cat then, intending to kick it across the floor, but it ran away, into the living room.

Amber followed the cat and found Peg leaning in the mouth of the dark hallway. She had changed into a red teddy-bear sweatshirt and a worn pair of corduroys. Her hair was pulled back with a cloth band, and her face was clean and bright pink. She was barefoot, her large square toenails painted red.

Oddly embarrassed by her injury, Amber hid her right hand behind her back. "Are you feeling any better?" she asked Peg.

"Yes, thank you," Peg said coolly. "Can I offer you something? A cup of Sanka, perhaps? An Archway cookie or a Little Debbie snack cake?"

"No thank you," Amber said.

"Did you meet my cat?"

"Yes," Amber hissed, pain pulsating in her hand.

"Shall we get started, then?"

Peg sat down at one end of the dark brown leather sofa and Amber at the other. Amber pulled the sleeve of her pale pink cashmere sweater down over her right hand and opened the small notebook in which she had written her list.

"Is your cat's name Fluffy?" she asked.

Peg shook her head.

"Is it Snowflake, Muffin, or Green Eyes? Is it Precious?"

"Nope."

Was Peg smirking?

Amber read all the cat names that might be appropriate for a white cat with green eyes: Casper, Smoky, Phantom, Ghost, Whitey. Then on to all the cat names she'd ever heard of, period, none of which was right.

She left Peg's house exhausted and hopeless.

Amber was dreading the following evening, but when she arrived at Peg's house, she found that Peg had ordered Vietnamese food, which Amber had never had before. They ate the delicious spring rolls and com suon nuong at Peg's gleaming teak dining room table. At work that day, Amber had compiled a list of names several hundred strong. *Maybe*, she thought, *the cat was named after a famous person*. That idea alone added two hundred names to her list.

After dinner, Peg, who was wearing a long sleeveless caftan that left her winglike upper arms exposed, ate two Little Debbie Zebra Cakes, while Amber, who had refused dessert, read from her list.

"Is it Tigger, Tiger, or Tommy Boy? Is it Eleanor Rigby? Tipper Gore? Ed McMahon?"

Peg shook her head. She pulled one layer off a Zebra Cake and lapped at the white cream she had exposed.

"Is it Olivia Newton-John? Cleopatra? Popeye the Sailor Man, Olive Oyl, or Swee' Pea? Is it Boy George?"

"Nope," Peg said. She shoved the entire bottom layer of the cake into her mouth.

"Dopey? Sneezy? Doc? Bashful? Bluto! Is it Bluto?"

But Amber was never right.

That night, she dreamed of a basket of white kittens. She scooped one up, and its mewling became a screech that made the hair on her neck prickle. Peg's white cat approached from a great distance. As it got closer, Amber could see it was really Peg wrapped in a white sheepskin rug. She was chanting something Amber couldn't make out. Then Peg threw off the sheepskin, under which she was naked. Her breasts swung from her torso like sweat socks filled with sand, and beneath her swollen stomach, between her tree-trunk legs, hung a pair of meaty balls and the thumblike stump of a penis. Peg was shouting in Amber's face now, her breath like feces, but Amber still couldn't understand what she was saying.

Amber woke in a panic, drenched in sweat. It was Friday morning. Her last chance. She called in sick to work and then sat on the couch in her fuchsia satin pajamas, frantically adding names to her list. The phone rang, and Amber cowered on the couch as the answering machine clicked on.

"Byron told me you're sick, poor thing," Peg said loudly against the mouthpiece, not bothering to mask her glee. "I hope you'll feel well enough to come to dinner. There's goulash cooking in the Crock-Pot. See you at six thirty!"

Amber had always thought of goulash as elbow macaroni and ground beef mixed with a can of crushed tomatoes, but Peg's goulash consisted of chunks of tender meat in a rich red paprika broth. She'd also made potato dumplings and a salad of wild greens with a mustard vinaigrette, and she poured a cold, fruity Zinfandel into Amber's glass. Amber ate as though it were her last meal. She'd barely had anything all day, having spent most of it calling every veterinary clinic in the area trying to find the one Peg used. But none of them had ever heard of Peg or her cat.

Peg couldn't wait until after dinner. "Are you ready, Amber?" she asked through a mouthful of salad.

"Ready," Amber said glumly. She opened her notebook. "Is it Cricket? Is it Sailor, Butterfly, or Potato Pancake?"

Peg shook her head.

"Is it Ashley, Victor, Victoria, or Nikki? Tad or Dixie or Adam or Erica Kane? Lily or Holden or Sammy or Austin?"

"No, Amber," Peg said, smiling and wiping her mouth daintily with a cloth napkin.

Would it really be so bad, Amber wondered, to call Peg once a week, to have a nice meal like this with her once a month? Maybe Peg would even help Amber redecorate her apartment.

"Is it Victoria Lord or Luke Spencer?"

"Nope."

And bowling might be fun. She was actually quite curious about Peg's teammates. For some reason she pictured them all as shorter than average, like Peg, their feet dangling as they swiveled in their plastic chairs, waiting for their turns. Amber watched Peg shovel a mammoth bite of goulash into her mouth.

"Is it Daisy or Petunia or Rose or any kind of flower? Is it named after a truck?"

Peg began to laugh. At first it was a low sound, wet and grating, like a hubcap falling off a car in the rain, but then Peg began to shriek and gasp. She inhaled deeply, and Amber heard a sound like a Ping-Pong ball being sucked onto the end of a vacuum-cleaner hose. Peg's eyes bulged even more than usual. She tore at her throat with her large hands.

Amber sat very still. It seemed that Peg had sucked a chunk of meat into her windpipe. The best thing to do was stay calm. Did Amber remember the Heimlich maneuver from high school health class? You felt for a certain bone and then pressed underneath it. Or above it. Or was that CPR?

Peg struggled to her feet. Her mouth formed some words—maybe "Help me"—but no sound came through. Inability to speak was one of the main signs of choking, if Amber remembered correctly. Peg tore the tie-on cushion from her chair and rent it in half. A few crumbs of foam stuffing fell to the floor. Amber rose, clutching her cloth napkin. Did Peg still have the strength to come after her? No, Peg fell to her knees, her face growing dark red like the goulash left in her bowl atop the gleaming table.

After a minute or so, Peg tipped sideways onto the floor, her head landing near the teak buffet. Her eyes remained open.

Amber sighed. It had been a long few days. With her napkin, she carefully wiped the wine bottle and the back of her chair. It would be as though she'd never been here, as though Peg had dined alone, as usual. For all anyone knew, Amber had been sick at home all day. In the kitchen, she washed and put away her plate, salad bowl, wineglass, and silverware. In the bathroom, she stuffed her napkin and placemat deep into the full clothes hamper in the corner and then paused to look at herself in the mirror.

Her naturally wavy hair, bobbed at chin-level, accented her strong jaw and large eyes. She was not only a very pretty girl, she decided, but a very lucky one. Byron would understand how the news of Peg's sudden death would affect the quality of Amber's work. One day off to recover, one day off for the funeral. She might even develop a horrible cold as a result of the stress.

As she gathered her coat and purse in the entryway, Amber thought she saw a flash of movement out of the corner of her eye, and her pulse quickened. Had Peg miraculously recovered, the chunk of meat dislodged by her fall? But it was only the track lighting reflected off the silver-framed photo of the white cat. Amber went to the bookshelves and wiped her fingerprints from each of the photos she had touched. She thought of the white cat's silky fur under her fingers.

Despite what the little beast had done to her, she couldn't leave it trapped in the house as Peg decomposed. If the body wasn't discovered right away, the cat might be forced to eat it. The thought made Amber suddenly dizzy, and she had to lean against the bookshelf for a moment.

When the room stopped tilting from side to side like a rocking boat, Amber walked to the front door and pulled the sleeve of her sweater down over her hand. She turned the brass doorknob and pulled the door open several inches. Frigid air blew through the opening, creating a swirling column of fog.

"Here kitty, kitty, kitty," she called.

Peg's cat crept out from under the teak table and stood considering her, its wide green eyes unblinking. Would it survive in the cold and snow? Amber wondered. Would one of the neighbors take it in? The cat streaked past her and out into the night.

Shoot, Amber thought as she watched it cross the street and disappear around the side of the neighbor's house. She never had found out the damn thing's name.

FIRE

For Lee Bradford

They brought him here the day he declared himself president of the college where he taught English. Going on thirteen years now, and the days only get longer, afternoons stretching like the white hallways into infinite nights. A dam with a constant high scream of electricity has been erected between his head and fingertips. He climbs the blue-leaved wallpaper, dreaming the journeys of his life: Canoe expeditions down the brown Mississippi from its source; dogsled tours over Minnesota snowfields, which he sees now peopled with white-lipped figures holding books. Rush of dogs, their warm breath rising in front of his eyes. And afterward, the fire, coffee, pencils, typewriter, the writing like fire from inside, stacks of scrawl and the bound manuscripts on his desk.

Later, students in rows, their eyes fastening him to the blackboard, awaiting the journey of words. His girls at home, lying on the floor with books. He feels their smooth hair under his hand. Now, he writes letters to his daughters with a fork in the potatoes on his plate but receives nothing in return, silence like the blank of his wife's face when he appears, snow-covered, at their door on Christmas Eve. She dials the phone as he sits dripping in the kitchen stroking his youngest daughter's blond, blond hair. The other two will not speak to him. The doctor and an orderly come to take him back, their faces pinched attempts at good will. It must have been years ago.

With the children, they visit the shore. They record it using a camera with moving film. Against the wall in his dark room, figures move, quivering vertically toward the water. The girls' hair glinting white where sun strikes. His wife in her dark bathing suit, her curls covered with a rubber cap. Slim and muscular, she can chop wood and tend the farm better than her father ever could. She teaches herself to swim from the pictures in an encyclopedia, then walks two hours each way to try the strokes in real water. Had he known her then? Hadn't he known her always?

Getting out is not difficult. In the dead hours, after even insomniacs have fallen forward in wheelchairs, he climbs the fence and walks to the lake. Sees it through the trees, shining dully like silver spoons tarnished with darkness. How he has loved the water, loved his body moving with it, through it. It will wash away the smell of singed hair, soothe his edges, which curl like a leaf's burnt brown as the year runs out, its fire growing smaller.

STOPPING BY

965 Sixteenth Street, April

J calls it boredom. Her sister, M, knows from adolescent psychology that boredom is just another word for age-appropriate restlessness—a squirming desire to burst out of the shell of useless skin, an urge to steal a car and take off across the river, beyond the ring of bluffs, in search of a place where you'll feel right. M and J snicker about the friendly reputation of their hometown, where people leave their doors unlocked and warm up their empty cars at the curb in winter. Where, if your clothes aren't right and your hair is sometimes dirty, if your mother drinks too much and works too little, then you are either invisible or the butt of a joke. M and J have few friends among their schoolmates, although M is certain she is smarter than most of them.

When they step into the living room, the man stops pacing. M lifts her hand in greeting, not wanting to disturb the baby in his arms. J crowds her from behind to escape the pool of cold air. The dim lamplight picks up the blond in the man's hair, which sticks up in front as though he's been pushing it back from his forehead. He wears jeans and a University of Wisconsin sweatshirt.

J stares at the baby's face, at its fat pink mouth drooping open in sleep. She has never held a baby. She imagines cradling it close, warm as a hot water bottle or a sun-soaked rock. In cold weather, the blood runs sluggish in her veins. *You're a reptile*, M has said.

When J looks at the man's face, he's smiling. His body has relaxed. He holds up an index finger and then disappears into the mouth of a dark hallway. Who does he think they are? M and J want to know, so they sit and wait on the microfiber sofa. The room is lined with built-in shelves filled floor to ceiling with books. In the corner, there is a thin silver stereo stacked on a table. J wants a house like this, clean like this, with gleaming hardwood floors. The apartment where she and M live with their mother has filthy carpeting, cardboard boxes half-full of belongings they haven't unpacked since the last move.

"Well, girls," the man says when he returns, "you just missed her."

"Who?" M asks, half-smiling.

She watches with pleasure as puzzlement crosses the man's face, a downward quiver of the eyebrows, before he digs a hole in his unconscious, lightning-quick, and buries his confusion there.

"My wife took Emily home about five minutes ago," he says.

J's stomach flips. It's exciting that he has drawn conclusions about them.

"She might even be home by now if you want to give her a call," he says. "The night is young, right? We're in for the evening. I guess the baby cried the whole time. He's actually a really good baby. You can tell Emily that. I hope he didn't scare her away."

"How old is he?" M asks.

"Four months old yesterday. Do you two know Emily from school?"

M nods vaguely.

"Do either of you babysit?"

They don't. M nods again.

J gets up and begins to stroll along the built-in bookshelves. When she glances over her shoulder, the man is grinning, asking M if he can get their number, but J can see he's nervous. She runs her fingertips across the spines of the books. Who needs this many books? Behind the man's back, she slides a slim volume of poetry from a shelf, T. S. Eliot, and tucks it into the waistband of her jeans, under her jacket.

M writes fake names and phone numbers on a pad of paper.

They skip out the door, down the steps. The wife is just pulling into the driveway, and they wave to her as they cross the lawn, the sidewalk, the street, waiting until they enter the deep shadows of the park before letting their loud dark laughter unwind.

Later, after M has fallen asleep in the small room they share, J slides carefully out of bed and, without turning on the lights, goes to the front door. She checks the deadbolt and slides the chain into place.

380 Campbell Road, June

The gate between the alley and the backyard hangs open on loose hinges.

M traps J's wrist in the cage of her fingers and pulls her in. She points toward the perfect summer scene—grass green and even as a pool table, the walk flanked by day lilies, allium, and bee balm.

"Oh, do not ask, 'What is it?'" M says.

"Let us go and make our visit," J replies.

They have memorized their favorite T. S. Eliot poem and quote lines from it all summer.

The sun has slid behind the roof of the house, but the wooden steps to the deck feel warm under their flip-flops. M turns the doorknob, pushes open the back door, and walks into a cloud of cold air, as though arriving at a great altitude. Behind her, J feels the breeze only around her calves and ankles, the cold current of a stream.

A woman with black-and-gray hair, the colors of burning charcoal, is standing on the other side of the kitchen island. The girls catch the clean smell of celery, and the woman pauses in her chopping, knife poised above the cutting board.

"Oh, hi," M says innocently. "Is Christine here? She told us to just come in."

"No!" the woman says, her voice high with alarm. "You have the wrong house!" She moves clear of the island, steps toward them with her arms out, as though to sweep them back out the door again. In her right hand, she grips the knife.

M turns to J. "Hey," she says, "you're letting all the cold air out."

J pushes the door closed and leans against it, the doorknob arching her back.

The gesture causes the woman to freeze a few feet in front of them, her eyebrows raised to create fat wrinkles that make her forehead resemble a bloodhound's. The cool air in the kitchen begins to thicken with her distress.

J is mesmerized by the physical signs. The slightly parted lips, the breath panting lightly, like a boy's when you kiss him. J's own breath quickens. The mixture of danger and other people's discomfort wakes her up, makes her aware of her blood pulsing. It improves her posture.

It makes M even smarter, this social-science experiment charting how people react when social norms are violated. She considers it fieldwork in psychology, which will be her major when she starts classes at the university, where she's been awarded a full scholarship.

She looks through the window that surprise has opened in the celery-chopping woman's psyche, as the woman considers the shelves in the psychic grocery store. What will she put into her cart? A blue box of Righteous Indignation? A red coffee can of Panic? An industrial-size jar of Hospitality packed in its own juice?

J wants a kitchen like this—yellow walls and stainless steel, a plant with marbled leaves draping the top of a cupboard, celery-scented air. There's another smell underneath that one, faintly garlicky—J's own armpits. She's ashamed now to have entered this clean, bright place without having showered, ashamed to think of the sink full of moldy dishes at the apartment she now shares solely with their mother. Can this woman smell her? At least she smoothed her hair down this morning and brushed her teeth. She jerks her camisole top up in an attempt at modesty, which seems in order here.

"What are you making?" M asks.

The woman glances back at the celery on the cutting board. M sees that she will answer the question because ignoring it would be rude. The woman's social training is kicking in, surmounting her elemental fear for her own safety. Slowly, she lowers her arms, and the flat side of the knife brushes her cuffed khaki walking shorts.

"Potato salad," she says grudgingly. There is a tremor in the hand holding the knife. Now that she has done the right thing, she is waiting for them to reciprocate.

Behind her, on the stove, the lid on a big metal pot levitates. The pot spits white foam. M nods toward it. "Your potatoes are boiling over," she says.

"Oh!" the woman cries, hurrying to the stove. She sets the knife clattering onto the cutting board, lowers the flame, tilts the lid of the pot.

J's eyes wander through an arched doorway to a room with a plump red couch. She wants to stretch out on it and watch television until dinner is ready, but she has a feeling the celery-chopping woman wouldn't approve. The woman would stand over her, frowning, as J flipped through the channels. The vision makes J angry. What has this woman done to deserve this house, this kitchen, this food, while J and M get nothing?

"Your friend doesn't live here," the woman says. "And it's time for you to be on your way." She scuttles sideways behind the island and picks up her phone.

M shrugs. "Sure," she says. "Could you just tell us which house Christine lives in?"

"Christine," the woman says. She purses her lips and narrows her eyes.

M can almost hear the woman's mind tick as she considers the possibility that she doesn't know her own street as well as she thought she did.

"I don't know anyone named Christine who lives on this block. What's her last name?"

"Jones," M says.

"Jones," the woman echoes. Her face turns pink. She doesn't recognize the name of someone who might live on her very own block!

M watches her try to decide between embarrassment and suspicion. If she chooses embarrassment, she'll be admitting weakness. If she chooses suspicion, she'll have to go back to being frightened by the presence of these strangers in her kitchen. Already her eyes are flitting to the door behind J, as though the girls are a vanguard for the drug dealers who are coming in next, to ransack her house.

"The Joneses would be hard to miss in this neighborhood, huh?" M says to J, who nods largely, eyebrows raised. M looks back at the woman. "Seeing as they're Black. And I mean really Black, like Africans."

The woman flinches, and M almost laughs aloud.

"You have the wrong street," the woman says tersely. She points her phone toward the door. "And so, goodbye, girls."

M sighs and says to J, "I don't know what we're supposed to do. I forgot my phone with Christine's number." She lays a hand on her stomach.

M has already received her first financial aid check and used it to pay the security deposit and first month's rent on a small one-bedroom apartment near campus. She's gotten a job as a cashier at Rudy's Drive-In. Four days to her first payday, and she has three dollars and half a pack of their mother's cigarettes. In the cupboard at her new place, she has two ramen noodle cups, one can each of soup and salty refried beans. Spin the lazy Susan at the house where J still lives with their mother and find five boxes of macaroni and cheese but no milk or butter in the refrigerator to make it real.

J stares at the platter of thick raw pork chops and hamburgers, at the pyramid of shucked corn on the cob, at the bags of potato chips on top of the refrigerator. Enough food for ten people. There are probably pies somewhere, ice cream.

The guests will arrive any minute. Someone will start the charcoal in the grill J and M passed in the yard.

M wonders what kind of story it would take to get this woman to invite two strangers to dinner. Is it already too late?

"Who's coming to dinner?" she asks the woman. "Do you have kids?"

"None of your business!" the woman says.

M wishes the guests would start showing up already so she and J could try to get someone on their side. Would it be enough if they broke down and cried? Are she and J too old to pull it off?

J watches the woman's gaze narrow as it moves over M's stringy hair, pointed chin, thin arms. People like this woman have everything, and they don't want to share. J approaches the island and wraps her fingers around a long pale stalk of celery. Her fingernails are short and dirty. The woman recoils, which makes J smile.

"Can I have this?" she asks.

"No!" the woman says. Her lips tighten around her teeth. She reaches for the knife once more and grips the black plastic handle.

J lifts the celery to her mouth and bites noisily through it. She chews with her mouth open while considering the tray of meat. She wants to grab two of the chops and two of the burgers and walk out the door, through the yard to the gate, but the woman has set her jaw in a discouraging way, and J knows she is on the verge of calling the police.

J turns away, yanks the door open.

"See ya," she says and steps outside, where the warm air is a relief. The woman should open her windows, breathe some real air for a change.

"Bye-bye, now," M says loudly as she pulls the door closed behind her.

Flip-flops slap against the warm deck, the concrete sidewalk. J lifts the cover from the grill and tosses it into a bed of bee balm.

"Fuck her and the celery she rode in on," she says.

M doesn't speak for two blocks.

"We could be eating hamburgers right now," she says finally.

"Dream on," J scoffs. "No way in hell."

"Keep your hands in your pockets."

The comment stings. In March, J was fired from the bakery at Festival Foods for scooping a fingerful of Holland cream from the giant industrial mixer into her mouth. So what? She washed her hands constantly at that job. The scowling bakery manager acted as though she'd stuck her finger in her ass first.

1219 State Street, August

A fairy-tale escape from the party on the first floor: a back door, a rear staircase, unlit. They climb through the darkness, clutching each other and laughing. The door off the second-floor landing is chained, so they climb on and find the third floor unlocked. Inside, a shadowy kitchen illuminated only by the streetlights outside. The girls can hear a television blaring to cover the music from the party below, which is so loud they can feel the vinyl floor vibrating with it.

M feels as though they have entered her own apartment in a different dimension. The layout is similar, but she has managed so far to keep her place tidy; she has even bought a mop. Here, the kitchen floor is sticky under their shoes, and the counters are piled with dishes. The living room is a moonscape; the light coming in through the tall windows illuminates the lumpy piles of clothes, bedding, and books on the floor.

The girls weave their way through the wreckage toward a bedroom pulsing blue light. They step through the doorway.

The room smells like a ham sandwich. In the corner, a twin mattress on a box spring, and in it, a young man propping his head up with one bent arm so he can see the television, which sits on top of a dresser. The man glances at them with indifference, pulls his free hand out from underneath the sheet. His hair is shoulder length and of indeterminate color, though it shines with grease, and his doughy bare chest is dotted with moles or acne.

M realizes, too late, that their appearance cannot possibly be a surprise to him, considering the rager going on downstairs. Maybe some of those drunken idiots have already been up here. She and J are operating without their usual advantage.

"Hi," J says. She perches on the windowsill next to the bed and stretches her bare legs out in front of her so that the man will be able to see the slender length of them out of the corner of his eye. "Why aren't you downstairs at the party?"

"I hate those assholes," he says. His eyes flash over to J and then back to the television screen, where an ad for McDonald's is playing.

M sits down on the floor and then stretches out on her side on the mat of dirty clothes that covers the carpet. "Why do you hate them?" she asks. She is annoyed by her own oversight, by the man's flaccid response to their appearance, and by the sexual desperation coming off J like heat off a grill. J would fuck this greasy-haired guy simply because he's ignoring her.

"I'm trying to watch *Star Trek Next Generation* here, girls," the man says. "It's one of the few episodes I haven't seen, and Tasha Yar has to fight this Lingonian chick, so if you wouldn't mind shutting the fuck up."

J can't believe he prefers a television show to two live girls in his bedroom late at night, and she says as much.

The man in the bed stares at J for many long seconds, his eyes moving from her freshly washed hair framing her triangular face, to her tits, to her long smooth legs. His eyes come back to her face.

"When it comes to women," he says finally, "I'll take fantasy over reality in a heartbeat."

J notices that her mouth is hanging open and snaps it closed. She looks at M, who is glowering at the man, speechless for maybe the first time ever.

Then M's upper lip curls away from her teeth in disgust, and J follows her gaze back to the man. His eyes are once again glued to the television, where two women, a tall blond and a curvy Black woman, have begun to fight. Under the sheet, the man is rubbing himself rhythmically.

J's face and scalp flush hotly. She feels trapped, as though she now has to stay till the end of the program. But M tips her head toward the door and releases her from the strange sense of obligation.

"Sociopath," M mutters as they pick their way through the living room back to the kitchen. J opens the door of the huge refrigerator and surveys its contents: a head of iceberg lettuce, a poorly wrapped block of cheese with dark hardened corners, a stout yellow squeeze-bottle of mustard.

"This is so boring," J whines.

She opens the freezer and finds a half gallon of chocolate chip ice cream—one of her favorite flavors—almost full. She pulls a large spoon from a drawer and begins to eat from the carton, which makes her feel less disappointed. She joins

M at the kitchen table, where she's filling in squares on a partially completed crossword puzzle with a ballpoint pen.

M represses the fact that her fury toward the man in the bedroom makes no sense. The episode has to run its course, and even when she knows the answer to the clues in the puzzle, she fills in her own words: *screw, you, Trekkie, asshole.*

J, who has eaten her fill, puts the cover on the ice cream carton and slides it back into the freezer. She finds a spot on the counter for her dirty spoon. She has been staying at M's apartment a lot— she finds living with their mother alone nearly unbearable—and M has been bullying her into cleaning up after herself.

As they make their way carefully back down the dark staircase, J says, "And indeed there will be time / To wonder, 'Do I dare?' and 'Do I dare?'"

"Time," M says, "to turn back and descend the stair, / With a bald spot in the middle of my hair—"

1017 West Avenue, October

The nursing home smells like piss and fear, like the veterinarian's clinic where J and M took J's little cat to die. M smiles at the red-haired receptionist and then proceeds down the long corridor with J at her heels. J tries not to look at the people contorted in their wheelchairs or lying flat on their backs in bed as though practicing for the coffin. She can feel the cancer growing black and nebulous in their lungs, livers, colons. She can hear the Alzheimer's worms eating holes in their brains.

Halfway down the hall, M and J slip into a room and pause just inside. A woman with cloud-white hair sits in a wheelchair at the window, her lap and legs covered with a red, white, and blue afghan. She turns from the window as though she has heard their breathing. Her eyes are glazed with blue-white winter ice.

"Hazel. It's Marilyn."

"And Jennifer."

"You girls. What mischief are you up to today?"

"Us?" M says archly, and the old woman laughs, high and hoarse and ending on a wheeze, her lips drawn back so you can see her gray teeth—her original set.

Hazel holds out her crooked shaking hands, and the girls step forward and take them.

They're so ugly, J thinks, looking at the knotted knuckles, the huge blue veins, the skin marred with brown spots. But Hazel's skin is the softest thing she's ever touched. She wants to stroke the hand, lift it to her face. She keeps hold of Hazel's hand even after M has let go of the other one. She tells herself it's because old people aren't touched enough.

"I like to sit in front of the window," Hazel says. She says the same thing every time they come. "I can't see anymore, you know, but I can feel the light on my face."

They first saw Hazel sitting in the same window just after J had moved in with M. She left high school just before her senior year began, enrolled in a GED course, got a job stocking shelves at Woodman's Market. Walking to the neighborhood grocery store near their apartment, past the long one-story nursing home with its row of windows facing the street, they noticed that only one set of curtains was open. There was Hazel, looking out onto the traffic on West Avenue, her face an invitation.

M stopped on the sidewalk and said, "I grow old . . . I grow old . . ."

And J answered, "I shall wear the bottoms of my trousers rolled."

They went inside.

Today they wheel Hazel out to the garden. The leaves on the trees are just starting to turn yellow and orange, and the sky is a thick azure. J carries a leather photo album from Hazel's room. In the gazebo, Hazel turns her face into the breeze and sniffs like an animal, reading the day. J opens the book of photographs.

M says, "Look at you in your horn-rimmed glasses."

Hazel wheezes. "Which album did you take, Jennifer?" She reaches out to touch the cover. "Oh, that's from the sixties."

"You're standing on the steps of a white house," J says. "You lived there way back in the sixties?"

"Before I came to live here, I lived in that house for fifty years," Hazel says. "On Vine Street."

J cannot imagine living that long, not to mention in one place. She turns the page.

"Here's little Carl in his pajamas eating breakfast," she says.

"Those grandkids liked to stay the night."

"Here's a screened porch with a green wicker couch."

"The kids and I used to sleep out there on the rollaway in the summer when it was hot," Hazel says, "to catch the breeze. We never had air conditioning."

"Who lives there now, Hazel?" J asks.

"Oh, they took it down. Students took over that whole area. While I still lived there, they tore down the house across the street and the house catty-corner from me, and they put up those cracker boxes and filled them up with students. In the summer, my heavens, they were loud. They would walk home from the bars using the most horrible foul language and pulling the pickets off my fence. What jerks, I always said. But Carl replaced all those pickets. He did such a nice job."

J feels the hollow hunger that lives in her stomach. She takes the photo of Hazel on the front steps out of its plastic sleeve. She's keeping selected photos in a shoebox at home—Hazel and her husband on their wedding day, Hazel and her dark-haired son and daughter as children, Hazel standing next to Carl, who is sitting on a red tricycle.

J stares at the image of Hazel's house. She wants to stand on those steps holding Hazel's hand, to sit on the wicker sofa and feel the breeze on her neck.

When M and J leave the nursing home, they walk the short distance to Vine Street, to the address Hazel has recited. They stand on the corner and look at the building that took the place of Hazel's house. It's long, tan, rectangular, with few windows. It seems monstrous to them in its plainness.

J holds up the photograph so that it blots out the new building, and Hazel's house is in the world again, white with green trim. Lilac bushes flank the front door. Inside, there's something cooking, something that could fill a person up. And there's Hazel in her horn-rims standing on the steps, welcoming them home.

HAUNTED

Eventually he and his parents moved away from the house in the middle of nowhere, the house with nothing nearby except the boys' reformatory that used to be a men's prison, but he still felt the ghosts of those boys and men knocking at the door as they had all those nights when he was left out there alone, felt their continued influence on his life in small, unlucky ways: for instance, they burned out the starters in all his cars—all of them—and gave shadows at a certain time of day a weight so that they seemed to lean up against him, hang on him, say things in his ears, and he was convinced it was them who kept him, even though he loved his wife, from lifting his arms and putting them around her.

CLOSE CALLS

With gratitude to C.

We're leaving to meet friends for dinner when the scanner on the kitchen counter squawks—there's been an accident on County B. Will, his hand on the doorknob, turns to me. We lock eyes, and I know we're feeling the same shot of adrenaline. We have a trauma kit in the back of our minivan, we're closer to the scene than the hospital EMTs, and—let's face it—being paramedics, we're better than they are. We'll beat them there, take care of things, and still have time for dinner.

Will drives, and I text our friends to let them know we'll be a little late.

The air is on fire out here, where you can get a permit to burn leaves. At the crest of a hill, we approach an older model Honda sedan from behind. Its front end is crumpled almost flat, and I picture the driver trapped in there. We won't be able to help until the firefighters work their hydraulics to remove the doors and push the dashboard back out. In the meantime, the local cop tells us what happened: the Honda T-boned a small cement mixer attached to a pickup truck that was taking a slow left turn into the driveway here. Turns out the driver and passenger in the Honda are both teenage boys.

Will and I exchange a look that says, *Maybe we should've just gone to dinner*, but we both know the only way that would have happened is if we'd been out of earshot of the call.

As the firefighters finish up tearing the car open, and we're able to get closer, I see that the car is crushed in more on the passenger side. When the driver saw the cement mixer in his path, he must have slammed on the brakes and veered to the left. If he'd been more experienced, he might have veered right, and if he'd veered hard enough right, with a little luck, he might have ended up in the ditch—a much better bet.

Will and I are on our way to get the gear from the minivan when the EMTs finally arrive. We introduce ourselves, our breath visible, multicolored in the bright lights of the fire truck and ambulance. As the EMTs survey the scene, I can see they're relieved to have the help. Will pairs off with one of them to work on the driver. The other EMT and I take the passenger, who is unconscious but breathing. I shut off the part of my brain that thinks of him as a kid and think of him as an object instead, as a series of observations and actions: Scan the body with my flashlight for blood and wounds: none visible. Count the body's ragged breaths, the fast, irregular pulse.

"Looks like a head injury," I tell the EMT.

She nods. Her scared expression reminds me of when I first started running calls almost two years ago.

"You're doing great," I tell her.

She'll learn how to cope just like I did—one call at a time. She hands me the C-collar before climbing into the back seat and stabilizing the patient's head. I position the collar and wrap the Velcro strap around it. Then the EMT lifts her right hand away, and part of the patient's skull comes along with it.

I start to see little yellow flashes at the edges of my vision then, like sparks in the heavy autumn dark that signal my own vulnerability. I clutch the car's empty door frame for a second and suck in the smoky air. Assessing serious injuries up close is vastly different from looking at photos in a textbook; still, I'm disgusted by my reaction and will never admit it to anyone.

The EMT's face is a glowing bronze mask floating over the back of the seat, and it becomes a touchstone for me as we wrap the patient's head in gauze, tip him out of the car onto a spine board, and slide him onto the stretcher. His right shoulder is lower than his left and strangely sunken in. As we secure the straps across his chest and legs, he twitches and struggles against our hands. A seizure?

We hoist him into the truck, and I leave the EMT to start the oxygen and IV. I look to see how Will's doing with the driver. These kids need to get to the ER now. Will and the other EMT are on the move, rolling the driver toward the truck. His plaid flannel shirt has been ripped open, and his lips are a deep red, as though he's just kissed a girl wearing vivid lipstick. I know if I tipped his head to the side, blood would pour from his mouth like red paint.

Will joins me outside the truck, combing his hair with his fingers as though he'll never get the style right.

"Ten one hundred," he says, the code for dead. "Torso's crushed." He reaches for my hand, squeezes it. "Good work tonight."

These words thrill me now as much as they did the first time he said them to me, back when he was one of my instructors in the Paramedic program, and I was the student who knew all the answers. I was married to someone else then, our kids just three and five. By the time I was certified and licensed, I was also divorced, and Will could take some credit for both.

We hold hands on the way to the car and all the way to the restaurant, avoiding the hard subjects and instead talking shit about the EMTs and the driver of the cement mixer. We share the details of the call with our friends, a married couple who work as a dispatcher and an ER nurse. They're good company, and the food tastes especially delicious—Will and I are both starving. Everything goes well until we're through eating, until Will excuses himself to go to the bathroom. As he turns away from the table, his smile flattens, and his face becomes the dark side of the moon. If we'd had a better outcome, the adrenaline high might have lasted all night, but now he's crashing, and I'm next. I'm in a sudden hurry to get home, put on Faith Hill and Tim McGraw's *The Rest of Our Life*, slip into bed with Will, and forget about the accident for a few hours.

I remember something then that hadn't registered at the scene: On the way to load my patient into the truck, I glanced to my left, down the driveway lined like a runway with solar lights, and saw a man leaning face-first against that dusty cement mixer with his hands clasped behind his head, as though he were under arrest or trying to block out the sounds of the world by clamping his elbows over his ears. He was moaning, and the sound wove through the static coming from the truck's radio.

DURING MY PARAMEDIC TRAINING I could finally be myself, without anyone commenting on my oversized personality or telling me to calm down. The instructors and other students had the same crazy energy I did, the same compulsion to run toward an emergency rather than away from it. We're not like ordinary people—that's what Will told me and a few of my classmates when we went for beers and lines of coke after our evening classes.

While I was taking classes, I waited until after the kids were asleep to pull my EMS textbook out of my backpack. I patted the couch cushion next to me, my husband Terry sat down, and I opened the book to a photo of a car accident or a serious burn. Terry gasped, covered the image with his broad hand. Then he slowly moved his hand aside, gradually revealing the figure on the stretcher, the paramedic in the process of intubation. I turned the page again and again, stopping at photos of puncture wounds and allergic reactions, twisted metal, misshapen limbs. As I went to turn the page, we steeled ourselves for what might come next. Sometimes it physically hurt to look at those photos, and we startled and moaned. Sometimes Terry couldn't look at all, while I was compelled to look closer.

Terry and I are opposites: He is mild and quiet, and I am excitable and loud. On our best days together, I fired him up, he calmed me down, and we met in the middle. But all of our arguments originated in the differences between us. As I became more myself, I realized that he was the antidote to my personality—one I no longer wanted. I also realized that if Terry and I had still been in love, I never would have fallen for Will in the first place.

My (admittedly self-serving) impression was that my kids, Ashley and Noah, and the rest of my family, even Terry, took the divorce surprisingly well. I would have sworn at the time that they all had crushes on Will—with the notable exception of my younger sister, Helen. She's Team Terry all the way.

I ran into her in our parents' driveway just after I'd filed for divorce. "Why do you think you're better than everyone else, Isabelle?" she said. She tossed her hair like some weird magnificent horse.

"I can't help it," I said, and she gurgled with rage and stormed across the lawn and up the front steps of our childhood home. All she's ever wanted is a sister who will take her seriously, and all I've ever wanted is a sister who will laugh with me.

IN THE MORNING, I reach out to the hospital to get the scoop on the boys, as I do after every call that nags at me. Turns out the local cops and emergency department workers know the family. The brothers were on their way home from basketball practice. They had both made junior varsity this year, and the older one, the sixteen-year-old, had taken it so well, was not angry at all that his little brother was as good a player as he was. They were best friends, born fourteen months apart. The driver was DOA, and his younger brother died overnight, around four in the morning.

The bottom drops out of my day. When I lose a patient, I always feel disappointed and guilty, but this is different, because I've never lost a kid. The news makes me sick—first just a profound uneasiness and then, by the end of the day, fatigue and body aches and nausea. I figure it's just a coincidence, that I must have the flu. My symptoms can't possibly have anything to do with the accident on County B.

But the nausea and exhaustion linger. Still I drag myself out of bed each weekday morning, put on my blouse, blazer, and pumps, and go to work at Dr. Blum's drab research office, where I've worked since before Ashley and Noah were born. As usual, on my off nights, I cuddle up with the kids, read to them, stroke their perfect rosy skin, and turn on their night-lights. Once they're asleep, I make their lunches for the next day. Lately, egg salad for Ashley, who is already nine and knows what she likes and doesn't give a shit if her friends say it stinks up the lunchroom. Seven-year-old Noah—thanks to my dad's influence—is nuts for braunschweiger with mustard on white bread.

One night, the combined smells make puking seem like a real possibility, and I'm hurrying along as best I can when Will comes into the kitchen. He's tall and built, with sky-blue eyes, and he saves people for a living. What's not to love? He comes up behind me and starts feeling me up.

"Isabelle," he breathes in my ear, "you have the breasts of an eighteen-year-old."

"Oh, babe," I say, "I feel so ill. Maybe I have an ulcer."

Secretly I'm pretty sure I've been cursed by witnessing the deaths of those boys out on County B. Secretly I'm betting I have cancer. Like most of the paramedics I know, I would rather die than seek medical attention, but I describe my symptoms to one of the ER docs, who shrugs.

"Sounds like a virus," he says.

"What's wrong with me?" I whine to my friend Jordan, the office manager at Dr. Blum's office.

"Is that a rhetorical question?" he asks. Then, "Why not just, I don't know, *go to the doctor?*"

Instead I grit my teeth and try to ignore it, even when I can't stomach my dad's sausage stuffing at Thanksgiving. Sitting in my parents' dining room, I regard my plate optimistically, but I can't stop thinking about the boys' family facing their first holiday without them. And the man driving the pickup pulling the cement mixer. Haunted for life, the ghostly moan coming out of his own mouth.

My kids are sitting on either side of me—Noah scooping burnished marshmallows off the top of the sweet potato casserole and Ashley humming a happy little song as she eats her mashed potatoes. I imagine losing them, and just a glimpse of that infinite hole wrecks me.

"Are you *crying* over that stuffing?" my cousin Randy asks, and then the eyes of everyone at the table swing toward me. They all want to know what's wrong. Will is holding half a homemade buttered dinner roll suspended in front of his face, his lips just parting to take a bite. When our eyes meet, his gaze hardens, and I'm certain he knows what I'm thinking. He gives his head a little shake, as if to release me from my thoughts. He reaches across the table with the roll, offering it to me, and when I bring it to my nose and breathe the yeasty scent of it, it smells good, as though I could actually eat it. I take a big bite and chew slowly, until everyone gets tired of watching me. Will and I have been in sync this way ever since we met.

I WORK ON THE AMBULANCE one night a week and three Saturdays a month, twelve-hour shifts. One mild Saturday afternoon in December, my partner, Vicente, and I get a call from dispatch that makes me break into a sweat, makes Vicente groan. It's a little kid, some kind of bike accident.

I pull onto the highway, take the exit toward one of the little towns in our county. We don't get many calls for kids, but when we do, it's usually bad, like the two brothers in the Honda. Every time I've brought up that call with Vicente, he's cut me off. His kids are twelve and fifteen, and he doesn't want to hear any details, which would only serve as fuel for the waking nightmares we all have about the accidents lying in wait for our own kids out in the world.

This call feels oddly personal to me: Why would I be getting another kid so soon after the last ones? What have I done to deserve it? The anxiety heightens my nausea to the point that I fear I might have to pull over and throw up.

On a side street, a woman flags us down. The patient is her daughter, a little girl about Noah's age. She's sitting in the mix of snow and gravel on the side of the road, attached by her right index finger to the chain of a bicycle, caught there like a wild animal in a trap. I'm beyond relieved it's not a head wound or a compound fracture or uncontrollable bleeding, and I have to tone down my sudden cheerfulness as I look into the mother's face, which is pale with terror.

She crouches, puts an arm around her daughter, and pets her snarled black hair, which is sweaty along the hairline, in spite of the cold air. I imagine the girl arguing with her mother about combing her hair, like Ashley used to. Ashley always outlasted me, and I would give up and send her to school with a rat's nest on the back of her head, which soon looked normal to me. Now Ashley brushes her own hair every morning without being asked, and it seems like a miracle. Kids have a way of wearing us down until their smallest effort toward civilized living is enough to bring us to tears.

The patient's face is red from the cold, shiny from crying. The mother explains that it's not her daughter's bike, which is at home in the garage with a flat tire. "She says it's Carmen's bike but that Axel was riding it."

Carmen, Axel, and the other kids are long gone, although at least one of them had the decency to inform the patient's mother about the incident. The patient can't or won't say how exactly it happened. The bike chain is way down near the base of her finger—she must have poked her finger through the hole between two rollers in the chain. And then maybe the bike started moving, because the chain has dug deep into the skin and flesh, which are now pulled up and away from the rest of the patient's hand; to pull the finger back out the way it went in would peel the skin and tissue from the bone.

When my hands approach the finger or the chain, the girl begins to pant with panic, her breath hot on my cheek. We have wire cutters in the truck's toolbox, but nothing that will cut through a bike chain. They'll have to do it at the emergency department. And then surgery on the finger. But right now, we need to get this patient into the truck and warmed up.

Vicente touches my shoulder. He hands me a wrench from the toolbox and then drapes a foil blanket around the patient's shoulders. I explain to the girl and her mother what I'm going to do. I loosen the bike's back tire and pull the chain off the hub. Vicente gently lifts the patient onto the stretcher while I follow with the chain. Vicente tucks another blanket around her legs, and I pile the chain like an oily black snake on top of her small torso, ruining her pastel winter coat, which we cut off in the truck anyway.

Throughout this process, the patient keeps her eyes on the injured finger, as though fascinated by the sight of it. Most people avoid looking at their injuries. This patient cranes her neck to watch her whole hand disappear as Vicente wraps an entire roll of gauze around the finger and the chain.

I strap the oxygen on the patient and examine the back of her other hand. There's a plump vein there that makes my mouth water. I rub numbing cream over it.

"Let's see, I'm going to guess that you're, what, seven years old?" I say to the patient, who is still staring at the big ball of gauze that is her injured hand.

She looks to her mother, who is sitting across from me, on the bench beside the stretcher. The mother nods.

"If you're seven, you must like knock-knock jokes," I say. "Knock, knock."

The patient stares at me, and I stage-whisper, "This is the part where you say, 'Who's there?'"

After a few seconds, softly, "Who's there?"

"Cows go."

"Cows go who?"

"No, owls go who. Cows go moo."

A small smile. Then I explain to her and her mom that I need to put an IV in her vein, to get fluids and pain medication into her body. The patient takes the news really well and, to my and her mother's surprise, she wants to watch me do it. I nod solemnly, but I want to laugh. The kid is destined to be in medicine.

She winces a little when the needle goes in, but she doesn't cry, and the medicine kicks in fast. Then she whispers something to her mother, and her mother's mouth falls open.

"She wants to know," the mother asks me, "if I can take a photo of the needle in her hand."

"Of course!" I say. I'll bet she regrets not asking for a photo of her finger before Vicente wrapped it.

Noah is seven now too, and his own little personality is blossoming, just like this little girl's. He and two other kids who live on our block like to call each other on their Echo Dots and meet at the corner to ride bikes around the neighborhood. He's reading so well on his own now that he doesn't need me for bedtime stories anymore, but I insist. The kids are at a great age, becoming more and more self-sufficient. While I sometimes miss how much they once needed me, I'm looking forward to the time, only a couple of years down the road now, when I can transition to working full-time on the ambulance. So long, Dr. Blum!

I'M SO WORN DOWN BY December that I finally make an appointment to see my primary care physician, Dr. Symanski, the week after Christmas. She tells me the last thing I expect to hear.

"Well," she says, slapping the test results down on the counter, "you're pregnant."

"*What?*" I am fully on birth control pills, without missing a single day.

"Birth control pills are 99 percent effective," Symanski says, "and you're among the lucky 1 percent."

I am stunned by this news. Before Will and I got married, I thought it was only fair to tell him that I didn't want any more kids. He was disappointed, even angry. He loves my kids, he said, but they're not his. He had to resign himself to the fact that if he married me, he would never have kids of his own. Seeing how much it hurt him, I understood when he asked for more time to consider a vasectomy.

"I guess I should have gotten that tubal while I had a chance, huh?" I say to Dr. Symanski.

"No one method is 100 percent effective," Symanski says, "not even tubal ligation."

She has discouraged me from the procedure because vasectomy is safer. I try to be a good sport about it now, at least while I'm still in her office.

Once I'm in my car with the door closed, I scream, "Shit! Shit! Shit!" until my throat is raw. On my way back to work, I plan my secret abortion, step by step. No one needs to know. It's such a relief when I decide I'm going to do it. Until five hours later, when I blurt out the news to Will as we're getting ready for bed, because I can't fight my natural impulse to tell him everything.

He stares at me for a beat, his eyes somehow brilliant blue even in the dim light, and then he whoops and lifts me in a bear hug until my feet are dangling above the floor. He starts to cry. Then he wants to fuck.

It's only later, Will asleep pressed up against me, that I start to unpack his reaction. He's happy about the pregnancy, so he has assumed that I'm also happy about it, in spite of our earlier conversations on the subject and on the subject of his vasectomy. Now, for the first time, I've kept my true feelings from him, because I know he won't like them.

"APPARENTLY PRETENDING TO BE Faith Hill and Tim McGraw in bed is particularly potent," I tell Jordan at work the next morning.

He laughs nervously and looks around to see who else might have heard me. Jordan is often nervous, but he also likes to joke around. He cracks us all up by imitating Dr. Blum, who puts a foot up on a chair when trying to make a point to us, his captive audience of office employees. This pose causes Dr. Blum's pants leg to ride high up his calf, offering a clear view of the thick dark hair springing over the elastic band of his black dress sock. He has a loud nasal voice with a trace of his native New York City still left in it, and as he intones whatever it is he thinks we ought to know—none of which we ever hear—he is also often tugging up the sock on his raised leg. When this happens, it takes all our restraint to choke back our laughter. Jordan's imitation includes putting his foot all the way up on my desk, which makes us all howl.

Jordan married a woman sixteen years older than he is, and while everything went well for the first five years, now menopause has plunged his wife into a bottomless depression and caused her to gain over a hundred pounds.

He hasn't had sex in three years, and he is really horny all the time. "Did you know that, historically, some women ended up in psychiatric hospitals during menopause?" he asked me during the first year, a hopeful expression in his hazel eyes. He's too loyal—and possibly too ethical—to cheat on his wife, and he has not worked up the nerve to tell her he wants a divorce. I am constantly trying to persuade him to do one or the other, cheat or leave, depending on the day and the attractiveness of our latest temp.

"What about this one?" I say, pointing to the comely young woman—dark hair and eyes, red-painted nails— sitting behind the computer just across from Jordan's office.

The temp looks askance at me, alarmed.

"What?" I say to her. "He's decent looking, don't you think? I know he's a little skinny, but he has the best smile." I pinch Jordan's lean side. "And he's a really good guy."

Jordan laughs nervously and pulls me into his office and closes the door. He collapses into his chair and tips back until the top of the chair scrapes the wall, and I lean on a precarious pile of papers on his desk.

"The doctor doesn't know if being on birth control all those weeks has hurt the fetus," I tell him. "It might have birth defects."

"Aw, Izzie, that sucks," he says. "When will you know?"

"Next week."

He's feeling sorry for me while I'm secretly hoping the fetus isn't viable, which I'm pretty sure makes me a terrible person.

By the time vicente and i get to the scene, the smell from inside the house has reached out and touched someone on the cold December air, a smell like a whole chest freezer full of spoiled meat. We're quickly overwhelmed by it, even on the front step. Whatever it is that's dead behind that door is communicating with us via molecules of putrescine and cadaverine: *Danger! Stay away.*

We go back to the truck, snap on gloves, strap on ventilation masks. Vicente stops on his way into the house to empty the mailbox, which is stuffed with catalogs and a few late holiday cards in bright envelopes addressed to Donna.

But Donna, I presume, is slumped in the bathroom doorway where she fell when she died, probably of a heart attack or stroke. There is no blood or other sign of trauma on the body. Her arms are at her sides, and her chin has sunk farther than seems possible into her chest. Her hair is iron-gray streaked with white; Donna is probably in her seventies. The skin I can see—on her face, her arms and hands, the stretch of leg between the hem of her pants and her white ankle socks—is burgundy, the color of raw liver. I look for a pulse as a matter of course, first at the wrist, then among the folds of the neck, where lines of pale skin mark the places the blood couldn't pool because of the way she fell.

When I stand up and turn around, Vicente is there, an inch from my face, grinning.

"Boo," he says, and I shriek. I can tell he's very satisfied with himself for having snuck up on me, even though he knows I'll get him back when he least expects it—once I've shaken this constant nausea.

Vicente calls the coroner's office, and we search the house for evidence of next of kin. On the mantel in the living room is an urn—probably Mr. Donna. Photographs in shiny metal frames crowd the top of the broad bookshelf: family portraits, vacation shots, kids' school pictures. Donna is certainly a grandmother, which I look forward to being someday. I consider how I denied Will the possibility of this lineage when I told him I didn't want more kids. But how much does blood matter? Won't my grandchildren be his grandchildren? Thinking about how he's put off the vasectomy for nearly two years now, I feel blood pulse in my face. I imagine saying the words to him: *I'm having an abortion.*

Vicente finds an address book in a desk, and I enter names and phone numbers into the form on our iPad.

"Pizza?" Vicente asks.

The coroner's lackeys might take hours to get here, and Donna doesn't care if we stick around or not.

"Ten-four," I say, although the thought of pizza brings me to the brink of vomiting. I didn't have morning sickness at all when I was pregnant with Ashley and Noah, not for one day, which is why pregnancy never occurred to me as the cause of my symptoms. "Do you want to call the family and tell them their mother has assumed room temperature, or should I?"

"I'll play you for it," Vicente says.

We play rock, paper, scissors, and I win with rock.

I HAVE MY AMNIOCENTESIS with Dr. Jones, who delivered both Ashley and Noah. I'm lightheaded with anxiety as she inserts the needle, and those little sparks of light appear again at the periphery of my vision. Will clasps my hand tightly, misunderstanding my distress.

"He's going to be okay," he murmurs. He's already decided the baby is a boy.

All Will can feel is happy, lucky. He hasn't noticed how I'm feeling—unhappy, unlucky—which takes a bite out of me. And, just like that, there's a space between us that wasn't there before. I feel abandoned and alone.

I watch the ultrasound screen as the needle penetrates the layers—skin, muscle, fat, uterine wall, amniotic sac—the hollow tip stopping just above the fetus curled up there in the dark. Dr. Jones draws the fluid into the syringe and pulls the needle out, and my uterus flickers on the screen at the same time a cramp grabs me inside. I can't stop myself from thinking, even knowing it's a myth, that the procedure itself might cause a miscarriage.

The fetus is positioned so that we can't see whether it's a boy or a girl, and I'm secretly glad, in case we lose it.

Later that week, we learn that the preliminary amnio results are normal. Will whoops again, lifts clasped hands heavenward, cries again, etc. And as much as I love him, in those moments I hate him almost an equal amount, because now I'm cornered. A healthy married woman in her thirties with a good relationship, good kids, a good job—of course she's going to have the baby. Of course she is.

WHEN I TELL ASHLEY AND NOAH that they're going to have a little sister or brother, they squeal and jump around on the furniture. Ashley, who loves babies of any species, rubs her hands together with glee.

"Finally," Noah shouts, "I won't be the youngest anymore!" But his face is set in a certain grimace as he bounces hard on the sofa, and I get the flicker of a sad memory: The week Terry moved out of the house, the nurse at Noah's preschool called, asking me to come right away. When I got there, Noah had that same expression on his face, and he was curled into a tight ball on the cot, weeping in great heaving sobs. He knows when something is being taken from him.

I announce my pregnancy to the rest of the family at my father's birthday dinner in January. Congratulations! Congratulations!

"Apparently Will has super sperm!" I say, refusing to meet Will's eyes.

A collective groan rises from the table, and my dad rubs his forehead to cover a smirk.

In the kitchen, my sister asks, "Do you think you'll ever make it through a family gathering without oversharing?"

I strike a thoughtful pose, index finger tapping my lips. "No," I say, finally, "I'm pretty sure not."

I love the huffing sound she makes as she flounces out of the room.

When Helen and I were kids, we sat across the table from each other at dinner, and whenever the mood struck me, I would open my mouth and stir the food around with my tongue, waiting for her to glance my way.

When she saw it, she would scream, "Oh! God! That's disgusting!"

I was about 75 percent effective at making her so mad she had to leave the table, and it still gives me a satisfying little rush to have that power over her.

WILL WHISTLES MERRILY through my pregnancy, throwing out baby names and coming up with ways to fuck around my big belly. I am nauseated and exhausted through the second trimester and then the third. Dr. Symanski tells me, unhelpfully, that sometimes pregnancy is just like that. I lie awake at night while Will is out at the bar after class with the other instructors and their students, getting drunk and snorting lines, and I mourn the death of my own ambitions. I'll have to stay at Dr. Blum's office for at least six more years, until the baby goes to school.

I consider the future of parenting with Will. He seems to have no idea what is coming for him, for us, and I don't have the energy to prepare him for what it's like to have a newborn. The closest I come is asking him to check how many weeks parental leave he can get from the college. The answer is ten weeks, and, like mine, it's unpaid, meaning we can't afford for him to take it. He has expressed no interest in the baby books I've checked out from the library and left on the coffee table in the living room.

DISPATCH GETS A CALL from a man saying his roommate is vomiting blood. Vicente and I ride to the address through the beautiful May evening with the windows down, inhaling the perfumed air as we pass yards draped in lilac, redbud, dogwood, magnolia. I'm resting my hands on my pregnant belly, which is straining the buttons on one of Will's blue work shirts.

We turn onto a street lined with rental properties. The house in question is in the middle of the block, the one with peeling paint, both the house and the trim painted the same Band-Aid tan. From the top step of the sagging porch, a fiftyish man, presumably the roommate, beckons. Vicente and I put on PPE—goggles, masks, and gloves—to avoid contact with the patient's blood. The roommate waves us up the steps and toward a sagging couch, where the patient, a slim guy of about forty, lies with his arms crossed over his narrow chest. The shaggy floorboards next to the couch glisten bright red. Vicente and I dig plastic shoe covers from our pockets and pull them on.

The patient is conscious and follows us with his wide brown eyes, but he is completely silent as we explain why we're there. I ask permission to check his pulse and take his temperature, and he nods once.

"Are you able to walk, sir?" Vicente asks.

The patient shakes his head. He does not make a sound or resist as we rock him back and forth onto a mat, lift him carefully onto a stretcher, and load him into the back of the truck.

Once he's inside the truck, however, he starts talking and won't shut up.

"You so horny," he says to me in a loud jaunty voice. I offer him a puke tray, and his long fingers close automatically around it. "Ain't that right?"

"We're going to get you some help now, sir," I say blandly. He smells like metal—blood and sweat.

"You want it right now, don't you?"

I look around the truck for something to put in his mouth. Would a roll of gauze be too big? I strap an oxygen mask to his face. "You might feel a little poke here." I stab him ungently with the big needle to start the IV, but he doesn't even flinch.

"You want to fuck a big-dick man, don't you?"

I slide the blood pressure cuff onto his arm and fasten it tight. I pump the cuff until it's surely pinching him, and I listen for the pulse.

Vicente, who has been taking down information from the roommate, gets into the driver's seat and starts the engine.

"All set?" he calls back to me.

"Hey!" the patient yells, the mask somehow amplifying his voice like a bullhorn. "Your girl here is tired of tiny taco meat! She wants to know what's it like to fuck someone hung!"

Vicente puts the truck back into park but keeps the engine running. He doesn't look back through the open window or even glance in the rearview mirror, so I can't tell if he's laughing or pissed off.

I wish I could think of something smart to say. There was a time I would have found it hilarious: a ribald man propositioning a hugely pregnant woman whose complexion is an abomination of hormonal acne, her hair hanging limply against her face, dark circles of sweat spreading under her chubby arms. There was a time I would have looked forward to telling Will this story and laughing with him about it.

But the truth is that I can't even look this patient in the face for fear that I will burst into tears. I feel defeated and so, so sad. I don't have the energy to keep up the usual wall between what happens during these shifts and my feelings about the people they happen to. This patient is most likely in end-stage liver disease, having drunk himself all the way to the sagging porch couch that apparently awaits some of us at death's doorstep. I know how resilient the human body is, how hard it is to kill, and it's difficult for me to imagine how much he must have drunk to get to this point. It is highly likely that he wants a drink even now.

"She's heard the news on the street," he says, "and she wants to find out is it true what they say about me. And I say, give the dog a bone!"

Finally, Vicente turns around, his expression carefully neutral. "You want to wheel, I'll heal?" he asks.

We trade places, but even when I get into the driver's seat, the patient keeps talking. "First she'll get down on her knees and suck my dick," he says in a conversational tone.

"Let's make sure you're securely fastened in here," Vicente says loudly, and in the rearview I see him yanking hard on the stretcher straps. Finally, I'm able to smile a little. He's a good partner. I turn up the radio.

THE BABY COMES IN EARLY JUNE. Will is there with me during labor, coaching me, his fingers laced with mine. This is the part he's good at. I feel so relieved once the baby's finally out of me, and from the second I hold him and stare into his cloudy eyes, my brain bathed in oxytocin, I love him more than anything in the world. Of course I do. A little boy, Casey William.

He looks so tiny cradled in Will's big arms, and Will's face glows with ecstasy as he looks down at his son. But on our way home from the hospital, my anxiety grows. It's one thing to want a baby and another to actually have one. That first night, Will surprises me by volunteering to take a couple of the nightly feedings so Casey can get used to the bottle and I can get some rest. Ashley and Noah love their new brother, and they take turns snuggling him and watching me change his diapers so they can learn how. My parents and Helen come by often during those first weeks to hold the baby so I can take a shower or a nap. Terry—who has always been a great dad, from the moment his children were born—spends even more time with Ashley and Noah. I start to relax a little. Maybe it won't be as bad as I thought.

Then comes the night Casey cries and Will doesn't get up to feed him as usual. I lie there listening, trying to determine whether Will is asleep or pretending to be asleep. When I can't stand the wailing any longer, I haul myself noisily out of bed and lift Casey from the bassinet.

By the time Casey is four weeks old, Will is sleeping through the night and slipping away sheepishly each morning to teach his classes at the college and run his paramedic shifts. He is going out again in the evenings with his colleagues and students. During the day, while the kids are at summer day camp, I spend too many hours comparing Will to Terry.

Terry and I had kids on purpose, and, as a result of that very conscious decision, I make concessions for the kids all the time. Once Ashley came along, I understood that my life was no longer my own. Terry helped me with that. Having a partner who is naturally nurturing, who understands the benefits of playing the long game, has helped me be a good mother. Will, in contrast, is the hero, not the ordinary person attending to ordinary details. He is always up for giving the kids rides to their friends' houses and cutting the lawn with the riding mower—the conspicuous tasks that people notice and thank him for.

It doesn't help that Casey loves his daddy, cries when Will hands him to me.

"I've got to run," Will says. "I have field training this morning."

He leans in for a kiss, and I move so that his lips land on my hair.

I nurse Casey, put him down for a nap, put away the dishes Ashley washed last night, start a load of laundry. I somehow never noticed before how little Will does around the house—much less than Terry used to. Ashley and Noah help more now with dishes, vacuuming, and cleaning the bathroom. If we can do it alone, why would Will help us? I find myself wondering if he's ever cleaned a toilet in his life.

Terry brings Ashley and Noah home one Sunday after an overnight, and I try to remember why we broke up.

"I miss you," I say recklessly, my lips trembling.

Terry's brown eyes grow huge. "Bye, kids!" he calls past me, and then he pivots and disappears out the front door.

When I next go into the bathroom, the mirror reflects what Terry saw: a crazy person with a splotchy face, red-rimmed eyes, hair puffy on one side and flat on the other. There is a crusty patch of yellowish baby vomit on the front of my T-shirt.

Jordan and I text and talk on the phone daily during my maternity leave. He has a real crush on the temp who is covering for me.

"Take her to lunch today," I say, although I know he won't. "You can sit in our booth at the deli."

"I'm afraid to ask," Jordan says, "but how are you?"

"Well, I've had about twenty hours sleep this week, total."

I can feel Jordan wincing. "Are you keeping track by carving little hashmarks on the wall?"

"And the minute six weeks is up, Will is going to want to fuck. At this point, I'm not the least bit interested."

"Wow, that bad? When are you going to tell him?"

"Not sure," I say, but I am thinking, *Never.*

SIX WEEKS AFTER CASEY IS BORN, Dr. Jones clears me for normal physical activity, and I start going to bed early and making excuses for avoiding sex.

"I'm sorry, it's still too painful."

"What did the doctor say?" Will asks, alarmed.

"She said to take it at my own pace."

Eight weeks after Casey is born, I stuff my sorrow and guilt way down deep and bundle him off to day care so I can go back to work for Dr. Blum. There, I spend an inordinate amount of time showing Jordan new photos of Casey—bald and toothless with buggy bright-blue eyes.

"Look at this one, he's smiling," I say. "Doesn't he look like the cutest little old man?"

Then Dr. Blum calls me out of Jordan's office to do some actual work for him—ugh—formatting the text, tables, notes, and bibliography for an article he's sending to the *Journal of the American College of Cardiology.* Then I have to go into a bathroom stall, hook myself up to a machine, and pump milk into plastic bags like a cow in a barn.

I'm looking forward to starting a new schedule on the ambulance—only two Saturdays a month, one day shift and one overnight, but I can't do more with the baby. Terry will take Ashley and Noah those two Saturdays, and I ask my mom if she'll take Casey.

"Sure," she says carefully.

We are putting away groceries in my kitchen, and an uncharacteristic silence spools out between us. I can feel her not asking why the baby can't just stay at home with Will during my ambulance shifts. The answer is that Will isn't really interested in learning how to take care of him. And I'm not interested in persuading him that it's worthwhile to know how to take care of his own child. And the real answer—the one I'll never admit to anyone—is that I'm punishing Will for not caring enough, for just going on with his life as if nothing has changed, when for me, everything has.

FALL SEMESTER, WILL TEACHES a Monday/Wednesday evening class, and after Ashley and Noah go to bed, I usually call Jordan. One night in late September, I describe what Casey is doing on his play mat—swinging at the brightly colored toys hanging down and twisting his legs from side to side.

"Has he turned over yet?" Jordan asks.

"He's so close!" I say. "But no, not yet." The kinder part of me doesn't want Casey to turn over until Will is there to see it, but the pettier part thinks it would serve Will right to miss it.

Jordan and I recap how, earlier that day, Dr. Blum accidentally kicked over the small metal garbage can next to his desk, and before he could catch up with it, it rolled out the door of his office and into the shared office space, spewing used tissues and plastic dental flossers and granola bar wrappers. One of us should have helped him clean it up, but it was all we could do to hide how hard we were laughing. The temp could not keep it together and had to rush down the hallway as if she were having a bathroom emergency.

Jordan announces that this latest temp, in spite of her appealing sense of humor, is too tall for him. He has been ruminating lately on his lack of sexual experience. He's convinced it's the main thing hurting his confidence with women, so I offer lessons in eating pussy.

"It can't possibly be as difficult as men make it out to be," I say. "Isn't that just an excuse not to do it? I'll whip up a PowerPoint for you."

Will appears suddenly in the archway between the living room and the dining room, and I stop laughing. I didn't even hear him come in.

"I have to go," I say to Jordan. "See you tomorrow."

Before the baby came, I would have gotten up off the couch to hug Will, and we would have cuddled up and talked about our days. Now I don't even bother to move my legs off the cushions so he can sit down beside me.

"Hey," Will says, and at the sound of his voice, Casey starts jerking both his arms and legs simultaneously in a crazy, hilarious dance, a goofy smile on his toothless face. Will scoops him up, lifts him way up in the air, and then brings him in close, kisses him all over his face and head. Casey rewards him with a strangulated baby laugh, and I have to steel myself against the warm feelings I'm having.

"How was your night?" I ask in a neutral tone. Even this feels generous to me.

He sinks down in the recliner across from the couch, bounces the baby on his knees. "A heart attack early on," he says, "and then a college kid with an allergic reaction. But everybody made it."

I can see how tired he is, the faint lines in his forehead and on either side of his mouth that will deepen as he gets old. I'm furious with him for daring to be tired.

"How's Jordan?" he sneers, flashing his blue eyes at me. That gets my attention. He knows and likes Jordan. Why would he say his name that way? "When's his first lesson in eating pussy?"

"You heard that, huh? What, were you eavesdropping?" The way he's looking at me, his eyes bloodshot and desperate, is giving me the creeps.

He pulls Casey close, jiggles him in his arms. He's probably regretting picking him up now, because how can he hand him off to me when we're arguing?

"Let's be real, Izzie. We've only had sex a few times since the baby was born. He's almost four months old. We used to do it *every day*. Now you seem completely uninterested in me. So who are you interested in? Jordan?"

"Have you lost your mind?" My entire body catches fire. The milk rises in my breasts. "I just had a baby. It's Casey I'm interested in. You were there with me, so you know how it goes. It literally rips you apart. And—news flash!—having a baby is a lifelong project, one that you seem *completely uninterested in*. If you think that holding him when you get home from work and feeding him while I'm on the toilet counts for anything, you're wrong! I don't want to have sex with you because you're a selfish asshole!"

The tension drains out of Will's body, and he slumps back in the chair, Casey on his chest. I can tell he's relieved to have admitted his suspicions. It's apparently been a real hardship for him to keep them from me. As for me, I've had it.

"You know what?" I say. "I want you to get out of here. Right now. Pack a bag and leave." The milk is soaking through my nursing bra now, drenching my shirt.

"Where am I supposed to go, Izzie?"

"I don't care." I unbutton my shirt, open my bra. "Give him to me."

A few minutes later, Will passes through the dining room with a duffel bag, and I don't bother looking up.

After nursing Casey and settling him in his bassinet, I ugly cry while wandering from room to room in the house Terry and I bought together. I managed to fall out of love with Terry. Has the same thing happened with Will? I try and fail to imagine finding my way back to him.

WILL CALLS THE NEXT DAY, and I make the mistake of answering my phone. He's staying with his paramedic partner—a younger single guy, probably the one he's been going for beers with—and he wants to know when he can come home.

"I don't know."

"You can't blame me for wondering about you and Jordan," he says, still not getting it. "You slept with me while you were still married to Terry."

"So . . . let me get this straight. You're saying, 'Once a skank, always a skank'? Is that what you called me to say?" I wait a few seconds, and there's nothing but silence from his end of the line, so I hang up.

HELEN SAYS, "WELL, THAT DIDN'T LAST LONG," and I can't help laughing, because I can tell she immediately regrets saying it.

My dad says, "Whatever you decide to do, honey, it's okay."

Terry knows that Will is gone, but the next time he picks up the kids, he doesn't say anything about it. He reaches out and puts his hand on Casey's bald head for just a moment, as though he can't help himself.

My mom hugs me for a long time, but I don't even want to look her in the eye, much less hear whatever truth bomb she's about to drop.

"Has it occurred to you," she asks, "that Will just doesn't know what to do? That he might be afraid or even just unsure of himself?"

It hasn't occurred to me. I have never seen Will in a situation he hasn't commanded. But I do know from experience that parenting is more difficult and more terrifying than the worst call. When paramedics arrive at the scene of an accident, we do what we can to stabilize the patient, and the rest is up to the doctors and nurses, the victims' families. We get to leave. But when you're a parent, there's no escape.

My mom hands me a piece of paper, a schedule for Parent Circles, a class at the community center for parents with babies.

THE HILL BOTTOMS OUT in a banked curve, and gravel crunches under my boots as I walk down the shoulder to where the motorcyclist lies. I can see gravel on the asphalt as well, and I'm sure his tires slid out from under the bike as he took the turn, probably going way too fast. I can see him falling in my mind, his body and the bike sliding toward the stop sign. He lifts his head as I approach, his handsome face clenched in pain.

"I hurt," he says.

I crouch and put a blanket under his head, which doesn't have a scratch on it. He isn't wearing a helmet. He is one lucky son of a bitch.

"Where do you hurt?" I ask.

"My arm and chest," he says.

"Are you having difficulty breathing?"

"Yeah."

He has probably broken some ribs.

"Okay," I say as Vicente jogs down the shoulder with the oxygen bag. "My partner's going to get you some oxygen, and I'm going to get you something for the pain and radio for more help. I don't want to move you just yet."

Vicente's face falls as he approaches us, and I don't understand why until I step back and pull my radio off my belt. My eyes travel over the patient and his bike. When I get to his legs, I almost gasp out loud. Somehow I haven't noticed until now that his right leg is pivoted in its socket, turned back and away from his body. He must have put his foot out to stop himself from sliding into the stop sign, and the forward momentum when his foot touched the ground rotated his leg like a doll's. The fact that he's not screaming in pain suggests that his femoral artery has been damaged.

I radio in with my back turned so he can't see my face. Then I walk back to the truck and return with a shot of pain medication and the iPad to collect the patient's emergency contact information. He gives me his husband's phone number first. If I can't reach him, I can try his mother, who is taking care of their three-year-old son today. I make contact with the husband, who, to his credit, keeps it together during our conversation, repeating the information in a clear voice as he writes it down.

"Do you have any questions?" I ask.

He hesitates. Then, "How bad is it?"

"It's a serious injury," I say, "but he's conscious, and his vital signs are stable. We've given him something for the pain."

"Thank you," he says.

Police arrive to block off the road so the EMS helicopter can land. The flight paramedics take a look at the injury and enlist Vicente and me to help move the motorcycle and get the patient onto a board. The four of us confer and decide there is no way to transport him without reduction—popping his dislocated hip back into the joint. We work together to sit him up and pivot the rest of his body around the injured leg. Then the first flight paramedic gingerly lifts the injured leg by the foot, stretches it slightly backward, and rotates it gently, in toward the patient's other leg and then out. He sets the leg down and shakes his head. The hip won't pop back into place, which probably means a fracture of the femoral head or neck. That means hours in surgery.

We help the second flight paramedic strap a padded KED around the patient's pelvis, roll him to his good side, and, finally, get him onto the board, onto a stretcher, and into the helicopter. It's the one of the longest calls I've been on, and I've learned a lot from the flight paramedics. As Vicente and I get back into the truck, I realize that I've been taking mental notes the whole time to share with Will.

WHEN I CALL THE HOSPITAL on Monday from work to check on the motorcycle patient, I learn that the neck of the femur was, indeed, fractured. The surgeons, after desperately trying to repair the damage to the tendons, nerves, and blood vessels that attached the patient's leg to his body, were forced to amputate it at the hip.

I hang up, suddenly so angry that I want to go to the hospital and strangle the patient to death. I have to leave the office, go outside, and kick a metal garbage can with my cute pointed pump. It really hurts, and I hop around on one foot for a minute and then start to cry. I walk to my car and get in and cry some more.

I've cried more in the past few weeks than I have in years, and I can't blame it all on postpartum hormones. Why would a man with a husband and a three-year-old ride a motorcycle too fast, without a helmet? Why would he ride a motorcycle at all? I don't know any paramedics who ride motorcycles— they've scraped too many bodies off the asphalt. Why would anyone take that kind of chance when there are people who love and depend on them?

It occurs to me that the fathers of my children have something in common after all: Neither one of them would ever risk his life that way. They are both well aware of what they have to lose, of what's at stake for their kids if they die. I dry my tears, grateful for them both, in spite of their shortcomings. And in that moment, a space opens up in my heart for Will. I'm amazed by the hope that expands to fill it.

That night, after the kids are in bed, I call my sister.

"Isabelle," she says warily. We don't talk much on the phone. Or at all, really.

"Helen, will you tell me the truth about something?"

"Uh . . . sure."

"I know you don't like Will," I say, "but do you respect him at all as a person? Or do you think he's just a total narcissistic loser and that my second marriage is destined to fail?"

Helen sighs. "Do I think Will is a narcissist? Maybe he has narcissistic tendencies, but I don't know that he could be clinically diagnosed."

I laugh. "That's comforting!"

"I don't think your marriage is destined to fail, Isabelle. Nobody's perfect, right? I mean, look at you."

She and I both start laughing then, and the experience creates a lightness in me I haven't felt since before that accident on County B that seemed to have set the events of the past year in motion. Thinking about it, I get a whiff of that burning autumn air.

I glance at the piece of paper lying on the couch cushion next to me, the Parent Circle schedule.

"Thanks, Hel," I say.

"You're welcome," she says, and there is such smug satisfaction in her voice that I have to throw my phone to the end of the couch before I give in to my impulse to cut her down to size.

Can the root of my issue with Will really be that simple, that I've been expecting him to be perfect when, in fact, he might not even know what he's feeling about fatherhood, now that it's real? But it's still possible that when I bring up the Parenting Circles, he'll have a list of excuses why he can't attend the classes with me, and it might really piss me off. Nevertheless.

I retrieve the phone and dial his number.

"Izz?" he says, and I hear the uncertainty in his voice.

JULIET

There was a boy the girl could not forget—so sensitive she thought she could see the shadowy bundles of nerve endings just beneath the surface of his skin. He lived in a rich house on the ridge, read Baudelaire, and in his bedroom made a tent with his mattress and box spring and slept there, over the heating vent.

The world seemed intent on keeping them apart. He called up to her from the dark yard, his voice entering her mind when she was supposed to be asleep or doing homework.

It's easy, he said. You just open the door and go.

It was one o'clock in the morning, well past curfew, when the police officer pulled them over on the viaduct for speeding. She went home in the squad car, and when her mother came to the door, squinting against the porch light, a little sound came out of her mouth, a sound like a flute, when she saw the man in the uniform standing next to her daughter.

What is it with you and that boy?

The boy came to her during the subsequent period of confinement; on Saturday night she invited him in while her parents were out dancing. Upstairs, in the glow of the red lamp, they lay together, listening to rain pattering on the leaves outside. She curved her hand around his neck, stuck her fingers through his brown curls as he told her a story: once upon a time, in a forest, there was a baby born with skin white as bone (he put his hand on her forehead, and her eyes fluttered closed), whose eyes turned from cloudy blue to the color of dark wood (his lips on her eyelids)—

And then her mother burst in downstairs, yelling a warning in a strange gurgling voice, as if the house had sunk into the sea with all of them in it. A slow-motion scramble for shoes and car keys, a jacket ballooned with air as the boy flew across the old matted carpeting, down the stairs. The near sucking sound of a screen door and the farther one of an engine, tires spilling water onto the wet street.

The girl's father tripped into the house seconds later.

Her mother had tricked him, had driven right past the house when they saw the boy's car parked outside. I'll kill him, the father said.

The girl's mother had insisted he get out of the car, to show her that he was sober enough to go home and confront the boy. Then she'd left him, driven away as he walked the line in the middle of the road two blocks away.

Now, the girl's father intended to go after the boy. But her mother would not give him the car keys. No, she said, and louder, No!

Upstairs, the girl clutched her pillow. She heard the scuttle of feet, a gasp, the sound of something heavy hitting the kitchen tile.

Downstairs she found her mother on the floor, her father bent over her squirming body. Give me the keys, he said, his voice deep and reasonable, his face red and crazy. The girl grabbed him from behind, grabbed whatever she could—an arm, a nose, the dark hair that would not move the head, it seemed, no matter how hard she pulled. She heard her own voice screaming. Saw her hand holding the telephone receiver, blood and skin under the fingernails. She choked out some words.

While the police talked with her parents, the girl climbed the stairs, looking for a safe place. She thought of the boy in his mattress tent as she curled her body into an oval in the small space between the bookshelf and the wall. Sometime later, her mind registered a voice and hands that pulled her to the bed. She heard the click of the lock on her bedroom door.

In the morning, she woke next to her mother and watched blue light enter the windows and move across their bodies. A cardinal began its throaty love song.

She could think of nothing but the boy's face, his tender, tender eyes, and what she would endure for his sake.

ACKNOWLEDGMENTS

Thank you to the Illinois Arts Council for their financial support of my creative work. I am also grateful to the editors of the literary publications where the following stories first appeared:

"Angels" appeared in *Parting Gifts*.

"An Easy Meal" appeared in *New England Review* and was a finalist for the NER Award for Emerging Writers.

An earlier version of "Signs of the Imminent Apocalypse: A–Z" appeared in *The Seattle Review* and was winner of the Bentley Prize for Fiction.

"Gopher" appeared in *Beloit Fiction Journal*.

An earlier version of "Moths" and "Paradise Is a Place with Plenty of Music" appeared in *The Good Men Project*.

"A Scuba Lesson" appeared in *Southeast Review* and was a finalist in the World's Best Short-Short Story Contest.

"Catalog" appeared in *Jane* and was winner of the *Jane* Fiction Contest.

"Romance" appeared in *Vestal Review*.

"Harmony of the Spheres" appeared in *RHINO*.

An earlier version of "This is Your Life" appeared in *Third Coast*.

"Peg's Cat" appeared in *Unlikely 2.0*.

"Fire" appeared in *Crazyhorse*.

An earlier version of "Stopping By" appeared in the *Chicago Reader* Fiction Issue.

"Haunted" appeared in *Southeast Review* and was a finalist in the World's Best Short-Short Story Contest.

"Juliet" appeared in *Reed Magazine*.

Thank you, Dr. Ross Tangedal at Cornerstone Press, for shepherding this collection through the publishing process. I appreciate your attention to detail and your creative flair. Thank you, Ellie Atkinson, for editing my words with care and grace. Sophie McPherson and Ava Willett, I'm grateful for your media and sales assistance. Carla Benton, thank you for your keen proofreading eye. This book is better for it.

Bonnie Jo Campbell, soul sister, thank you for being such a generous friend, critic, and fellow traveler on this bookish path. Andy Mozina, thank you for helping me attend to the big picture and the plot, even when magic is involved. Thank you, Jaimy Gordon, for your invaluable notes on these stories, both in the past and more recently. The influence of your teaching is all over them. Nancy Peterson, thank you for showing up at exactly the right time to lend your knowledge to these stories, and for taking such care with my writing and with me. Thank you, Matthew Salesses, for hearing me and believing in my work. Thank you, Carla Vissers, for helping improve many of these stories over the years. Thank you to the nonwriters who shared their stories with me, even when warned that I might write them down.

To the warm and elegant publicist Sheryl Johnston, thank you for applying your considerable skills to guiding this book in the world. I'm lucky to know you.

Lorna Crowl, I'm grateful for the healing work we do together. Relatedly, thank you to the stewards of the Forest Preserve District of Kane County—these wild places are vital to my health.

Thank you to my parents, Nancy Thomas-Kremmer and Bill Bell, for passing down the love of a good story. Thanks to my siblings—Tania Taff, Barbara Brown, and James Bell—and their spouses, kids, and grandkids for their love, humor, and good company. Thank you to my in-laws, the Burkes and Nowickis, for their enthusiasm and support.

Most of all, thank you, Adam Burke—tender partner, first reader, staunchest advocate, favorite person—for walking with me, through thick and thin.

HEIDI BELL is an award-winning writer and editor. Her short fiction has appeared in many literary publications, including *Crazyhorse, New England Review, The Good Men Project*, the *Chicago Reader, Southeast Review*, and *The Seattle Review*, where she won the Bentley Prize for Fiction. She is the recipient of two Illinois Arts Council Fellowships in Literature. She lives in Aurora, Illinois.